THE DATE DARE

TARA SUE ME

PRAISE FOR THE DATE DARE

"*The Date Dare* is a sweet friends-to-lovers romance, with great characters, an interesting plot twist that will keep you stick to the book until the very end"

— COLLECTOR OF BOOK BOYFRIENDS

"With a pinch of turmoil and a heaping handful of steamy chemistry, this was a romance I could savor!"

— JEWLS BOOK BLOG

"One of my favorite reads this year!"

— CAROLINA CHICS READ

This is an updated version of THE DATE DARE published in 2018.

Publication Date: November 21, 2019

Cover image: istock

Editor: Sandra Sookoo

ISBN ebook: **9781950017133**

ISBN print: 9781950017003

CHAPTER ONE: DARCY

"SOMETIMES GOOD THINGS FALL APART SO
BETTER THINGS CAN FALL TOGETHER."
MARILYN MONROE

*E*lliott and I have been best friends since Kindergarten, so I don't think it's a stretch to say I probably know him better than anyone. However, I have never been able to figure out why he dates the women he does.

Take for example the one he's with tonight. First of all, it's the World Series and Atlanta is playing. Elliott and I always watch the finals when they're in it. Granted, it's been several years since they've made an appearance, but it'd take more than a hot date to keep him away from my place tonight.

It's fairly obvious his date, the second woman he's dated this October and henceforth referred to as O2, wasn't made aware of Elliott's plans prior to their arrival. Not with the way she's leaning against the table examining her nails and the dagger of ice glare she shoots him with every five minutes. Elliott is, of course, clueless. But that's Elliott for you.

He probably thinks the skintight dress she's wearing is fine for an evening of baseball and beer. More than likely,

1

he's perfectly content to wait until after the game to peel the red fabric off her, but O2 is not. She wants Elliott and she wants him *now*.

Not that anyone can blame her. I'll be the first in line to admit Elliott is one of the best looking men I've ever seen. And thanks to his job as a trainer for the state's professional lacrosse team, the Georgia Storm, his body is pretty fantastic, too. Of course, that's my opinion based solely on my imagination and what I can infer from the way he wears his clothes. I, unfortunately, haven't seen him naked since we were six.

So yes, Elliott's a catch and a half, and any woman would be proud to be on his arm. And yet, he keeps going out with these plastic lookalike women.

I skirt past O2 and sit on the couch beside him. "O2's a little overdressed, isn't she?" I ask, reaching across him to grab a handful of chips.

"Her name is Alice," he says, keeping his eyes on the television.

"She makes it to November, she'll be Alice. Until then, she's O2."

"Don't let her hear you call her that. I don't feel like explaining your naming system to my date."

His voice is sharper than normal and I look at him in shock. He's not actually serious about this one, is he? He's frowning, but he's not angry. "What crawled up your ass today?" I ask. I've been refusing to learn the names of his women for at least the last year and he's never minded. I glance over my shoulder to see what this latest one is up to. She's chatting with Richard, one of the players Elliott works with.

I actually end up watching her for a few minutes and not once does she ever turn her head toward Elliott. She's completely caught up in her conversation. At one point, Richard says something and she laughs this horrible sounding laugh that is part hyena and part strangled cat.

Then, right there in my kitchen with God and half the Storm players present, she runs a perfectly manicured nail down the guy's chest. Now I've never mastered the fine art of lip reading, but I'm pretty good at interpreting body language and her body wasn't so much saying, *You must excuse me so I can go sit with my date* but rather, *Let's blow this joint so I can blow you.*

I'm not sure if Richard knows she came with Elliot. I'd like to think not. In the Utopia I've created in my brain, work friends do not walk around with their hand on your date's ass. But then again, I work in the hotel industry and Elliott works with professional athletes. I know from previous conversations with him that a few members of the team are into some pretty kinky shit, so I don't know, maybe they do.

But when I glance back at Elliot, he's watching them with a look that is so raw and vulnerable that I swallow the smart-ass comment I'm about to say and put my hand on his knee.

"You deserve better, Elliott Taber," I whisper, so no one hears, but the game is back on following a commercial break and no one is paying us any attention anyway.

He shakes his head and looks surprised for a few seconds. It's almost as if he'd been asleep and I woke him up. "What?" he asks.

I nod to the corner of the kitchen where Richard and O2 are trying to make out without being obvious they're making out. Which really means they're standing in the corner of my kitchen and being all handsy when they think no one's watching.

"I was just saying you deserve better than O2 over there. I mean, really? What's she doing hanging all over him when she came with you?" I suddenly can't stand the sight of them anymore so I turn back to face him. "She's a guest in my house. I have a good mind to kick her out."

"Don't worry about those two. I'm not." His expression is back to his usual carefree and easy one.

I'm floored at how calm he's acting and it's causing me to grow more and more concerned about his state of mind. How can he sit there like it's nothing while his date is climbing all over another man who also happens to be his work associate?

"You're entirely too calm about this," I tell him. "It's not normal."

He sighs deeply right as a chorus of cheers go up around us, and we both realize we're missing a good part of the game. I check the score and give the guy sitting on the other side of me a high five.

Elliott leans over to me. "We don't have a normal relationship," he says in a low voice.

"What do you mean by that?" His eyes are hazel, with flecks of gold and green. I've always thought they were cooler than my boring blue. "How many people do you know that have been friends for twenty-five years?"

His gaze is steady. "I wasn't talking about me and you."

"Then who were you talking about?"

Another cheer goes up and Elliott brushes me off. "We'll talk about it later. Come on. Let's watch the rest of the game."

Our conversation isn't finished, and he knows this. But I agree that this isn't the best place or time to talk. Besides, if he wasn't talking about our relationship, then he had to have been talking about him and O2. And if there was any

4

relationship I don't want to talk about while my boys win the World Series, it's that one.

For the next few hours, we fall back into our old and comfortable routine of yelling at the players and the umpires. We eat way too much, drink way too much, and laugh way too loud. In other words, good times.

When the game ends and people begin to leave, I look around and both O2 and Richard are gone. Elliott shrugs like it's no big deal, but I'm not going to let him get away with it that easily.

As it so happens, I'll be staying in Atlanta for an extended period of time. Typically, with my job as a brand expert with an international hotel chain, I'm only in my home city for two weeks out of the month. Since the season has just ended for the Storm, Elliott will be around as well. It'll be the perfect occasion for me to finally get to the bottom of what the hell his problem is with women.

"Looks like O2 left your sorry ass," I say with a punch to his arm when almost everyone has left other than him.

"*Alice* and I have an understanding." His smile is back in place, but it doesn't make it to his eyes.

I can't imagine a couple with any sort of relationship that finds it acceptable for one person to leave the other in the middle of an evening out, but whatever. He can attempt to explain it to me later.

"You and me," I tell him. "Tomorrow night. The Barn. Seven o'clock. O2 isn't invited and you best not even think of bringing O3." It's our favorite steak house, so he'll show up.

He tells the remaining guys and their dates goodbye, all the while acting like he didn't hear me.

. . .

5

HE STEPS OUTSIDE for a minute to call a driving service to pick him up and he's frowning when he comes back in. "They're slammed and it'll be thirty minutes before they can be here. I should have realized with the game and all it'd be that way and called earlier."

"That's okay," I say with a wink. "Now you can help me clean up."

"Is that a horn I hear?" He cups a hand to his ear. "They must have estimated incorrectly how long it'd take to get here."

I roll my eyes. "Good try, but not good enough. Grab those bags of chips, will you?"

Elliott and I have been friends for so long, we work seamlessly together. We don't even have to talk, but fall naturally in place beside the other. Within twenty minutes everything has been put away and wiped down.

"Excellent," I say, looking around. "All I need to do now is vacuum and I'll take care of that in the morning. That car service should be late more often."

"Speaking of, they should be here soon. I'll go wait outside." He shoves his hands in his pockets. "Tomorrow night. Seven. The Barn. Did I forget anything?"

He's teasing me so I walk to where he's standing and punch his shoulder. "You. Only you, and no date."

"Right. That was it. You've got it." He leans down and kisses my cheek. I don't think it's my imagination that he hesitates a second longer than necessary. "Just me," he whispers and pulls away.

He's gone and out the door before I realize I'm standing in my doorway with a hand on my cheek, lightly touching the place his lips had been seconds before.

CHAPTER TWO: ELLIOTT

"WOMEN ARE MEANT TO BE LOVED, NOT
TO BE UNDERSTOOD." OSCAR WILDE

*W*hen I was in college, my roommate asked me if it was weird having a best friend who was a girl. I wasn't sure how to answer the question. Darcy had always been my best friend and she'd always been a girl. I finally told him no and weird would be having a guy as my best friend.

That was when my eyes opened and I realized how rare it is to have a relationship like the one Darcy and I share. With her, I'm Elliott and she's Darcy. We don't have to apologize for anything and we don't have to hide anything.

But I *am* hiding something from her.

Life is funny. You always think it's the big moments, the ones with lots of pictures and fanfare that are the great turning points. Not so for me.

Mine was last year's Holiday Charity Ball the Storm organization puts on each December. Darcy was my date, as per usual, because she loves getting dressed up as much as I hate it. Plus, not only is she hot as hell, she won't act all weirded out to be in the public eye with a bunch of pro athletes. Trust me on that last one, it's a lesson I learned the hard way.

We were entering the hotel behind a player who had captured the city's love and devotion by completing a seemingly impossible move to cement a win. The security guards were keeping the general public a good distance away, but a young boy ran up to this guy and asked for an autograph. The player was all smiles and proceeded to kneel at the boy's level and talk with him. This was the shot all the newspapers and TV newscasters went crazy over.

But not me.

The boy's mother and little sister were back away from the crowd and closer to where Darcy and I stood completely unnoticed. Even the boy's mom had her attention focused on her son. Truth be known, it was where my focus was as well.

Until I turned to see if Darcy happened to have her phone out so I could ensure we had a shot from our unique perspective. She did not. She had no interest in the boy or the famous athlete or anything the rest of those present were watching. Because Darcy was playing Peek-a-Boo with the boy's younger sister.

It wasn't like I'd never seen her do it before. I had. But somehow, something about that moment struck me inside and I knew I'd never recover. There she was, dressed to the nines in a gorgeous black designer gown, her long brown hair in an elegant upsweep, and pearls she'd borrowed from a friend, drawing attention to her slender neck. She's standing slightly bent at the waist so she could get somewhat eye level with her audience, and playing Peek-a-Boo with a baby.

The autograph was finished, people started moving

forward again, and the mother with her two children in tow walked away. Darcy took my arm and tilted her head.

"Are you okay?" She asked, her blue eyes filled with concern.

"Yes, I'm fine. Just a bit chilly." It was surprising how easily the lie had slipped out, but what was I supposed to do? Tell her I'd fallen in love with her in a single moment?

Not likely.

TRUE TO FORM, Darcy is waiting for me when I arrive at the restaurant the following evening. Her absolute refusal to ever be late anywhere is a trait of hers I accepted years ago. But tonight as I slide into the booth to sit across from her, she quickly covers up a look of surprise.

I raise an eyebrow. "Are you shocked that I'm here or that I came alone?"

"I knew you wouldn't stand me up."

Interesting. She thought I'd bring someone with me tonight? I don't have time to contemplate why that is before she answers as if I asked the question out loud.

"You do realize that this is the first time in almost a year that you haven't brought a date along when we're doing something together?"

Surely she can't be right, but her words echo in my head and I don't need a calendar to know she's correct. I haven't put myself in a position to be alone with her since the charity ball last December.

"I guess I hadn't realized that," I say. "I'm sorry, Darcy. Truly." Though what I'm apologizing for, I'm not sure. I don't think it's a good idea for me to be alone with her because I'm afraid I'll slip and she'll know how I really feel about her. Along those same lines, I'm not going to apologize for falling in love with her because that's just stupid. Maybe I'm apologizing for not having the balls to tell her how I feel. I don't know.

I don't realize I'm digging my fingers into my hair until she reaches across table and gently touches my arm.

"Elliott," she says, and I don't deserve the concern in her eyes. Not when it's only there because I'm too scared to tell her how I feel. "Hey, I'm worried about you."

I take her hand. "I'm fine, Darc," I say, using an old nickname I haven't used in years. It's unexpected and her cheeks flush. I run my thumb over her knuckles, hoping to soothe her a bit and because I love the feel of her skin. "I'm stressed out, that's all."

She's a smart woman and she's aware it's more than that. But she's also my best friend and she knows when not to push. "Okay," she says, pulling her hand away because right at that moment the waiter comes to take our order. Even so, I miss her touch.

When he leaves, she thankfully changes the subject, but I'm not sure the new direction is any better. "Tell me what you were talking about last night when you said you weren't normal."

"I meant Alice and I were never in a normal relationship."

"After she left your ass high and dry last night, I would hope you're not in any sort of relationship with her." She raises an eyebrow as if to say, *You know I'm right.*

"Our time together was based on a mutual agreement to fulfill specific needs the other person had." I'm hoping she'll let me leave it at that, but it's unlikely since I can almost see her brain working through the meaning of my words.

I silently plea with her to let it go and when our salads are brought to the table, I think I might get a reprieve.

However, no sooner is the server gone, than she levels her gaze back my way. "Explain, please."

I think about making it sound prettier than it is, but fuck it, I'm talking to Darcy. Seriously, she knows all my dirty little secrets.

Except for one.

Still, I'm a bit hesitant with my reply, so I say it completely devoid of any emotion. "I had a need to get laid and she had a need to meet some professional athletes." It's shallow, but the truth.

"Are you serious with that answer?"

"Did I stutter?"

"Oh my, God, I can't believe you." She puts her fork down and leans across the table. "You are, aren't you? You're completely serious."

I shrug. I'm fairly certain there was nothing joking in the way I answered. "Is that a rhetorical question or are you expecting an answer?"

"You know this is not normal, don't you?"

"I believe I said as much last night," I say and hope she drops it soon.

"No. I mean this is way, way, way beyond normal." She picks up her fork and takes a bite of salad.

It's always made sense to me. After all, I do have needs and the woman I love isn't going to take care of them since she doesn't know I love her. What am I supposed to do?

Of course I can't tell her that.

I've suddenly lost my appetite, and I should say something to convince her I've not gone off the deep end or to steer the conversation toward a less volatile subject. Unfortunately, at the moment, I have no idea how to do either.

This is why I never meet with her alone anymore,

because I knew as soon as I did, this very thing would happen. I'm surprised she isn't seeing right through me and picking up on exactly what my problem is. It's so hard to always be on high alert, making sure my tone doesn't give anything away, or that my touch doesn't linger.

She gasps and my heart stops. Fuck. She does know. I take a deep breath and tell myself I can do this. I can confess my feelings about her and we'll take it from there. She won't feel the same, but it's not like she'll stop being my friend.

It'll be okay.

I hope.

"You know what your problem is?" she asks, slightly titling her head.

"No," I reply because now I'm thinking it'll be better if she says it first.

"You've been dating the wrong type of woman."

Of course I am, because none of them are you.

I don't say it, but I think it. In fact, I don't open my mouth at all for fear those exact words will come spilling out on their own.

"Well?" She asks proudly and crosses her arms over her chest like she's waiting for me to give her a round of applause.

"I don't think I'd describe the arrangement Alice and I had as dating."

"You're right," she says. "Let me rephrase. You need to start dating the *right* type of woman."

There is no way I can argue that. She's absolutely correct. Unfortunately, it's not about finding the right type of woman, because there's only one woman for me. Except she doesn't know that. So for now, I play along with her like the coward I am.

I sit back in my seat. "And I suppose you know the right type of woman that I should date?"

"Of course I do," she says with the confident smile I love so much and my heart warms. "I know everything about you. I know you better than you know yourself."

I don't doubt her, but I want to mess with her a little bit. "Oh you do, do you?"

"Oh, yes, absolutely."

She looks so sure of herself, and I shouldn't do what I'm getting ready to do. Unfortunately, I can't help myself. "Okay Miss Smarty-pants, when I'm eating pussy, do I prefer the woman to be lying down, sitting on my face, or ewww gross, people do that?"

She tries to cover her surprise at my question but she's not completely able to. Is she picturing us together the way I am? I can't tell. Although I have to hand it to her, she recovers pretty quickly and answers, "It better not be the last one."

I can't help but to smile at her response. "I'll give you that much, it's not. But tell me, which of the others is it?"

She's actually thinking about it and when her cheeks flush pink, I'm pretty sure she *is* imagining me between her parted thighs and I'm instantly hard. "Lying down?"

"No." I lean forward. I don't think anyone's listening, but I need to ensure they can't hear what I'm about to say. The flush of her cheeks has made me bold. "I want you on my face. I've found that's the best way to both taste you and to get my tongue inside you the deepest. Although, granted, I'm not really picky and I'll eat your pussy anyway you give it to me."

Her mouth is still open when I continue, "Next question. When you take me in your mouth do I let you lead or do I hold your head still while I fuck your face?"

13

She glides her gaze down my body. With the way we're sitting she can't see anything, but I still shift in my seat because suddenly my dick is doing all it can to bust out of my jeans and flag her down. Her fork clatters to the table.

"Ummm." She looks everywhere except me. "You'll let me lead."

"No. I'm pretty much fifty, fifty on that one. Could go either way, depending on the day and my mood."

She slinks into the seat with a low groan. I think about stopping, but decide to keep going. I have to know how far she'll let me go.

"Next one," I say.

She holds up a hand. "I think that's enough. I said date you, not fulfill all your sexual needs."

"If she's the right woman for me, they're one and the same."

"This entire line of questioning is stupid. I said I could find the right type of woman for you to date. I wasn't talking about knowing you like that. Besides, I doubt you know *my* sexual preferences."

I should take her at her word and shut up. I should stop while I'm ahead, and let it die. If I was smart, if I had a brain in my head, if I wasn't so into knowing her deep dark secrets I would. But I can't. Looking into her eyes, I tell her, "I know you won't sleep with anybody before the fifth date. I know you like a lot of foreplay because you think it's hard for you to come. But in reality, I don't think you've ever been with a man who turned you on that much. I know you like dirty talk while you're fucking and you like to cuddle and kiss afterward." The image of her, soft and sated, in my arms is too much and I have to pause for a breath before adding in a whisper, "And I think somewhere deep inside you fear you'll never find a man who can satisfy you."

14

By the time I finish talking, her mouth is wide open in utter and complete shock. All I can think is how badly I've fucked up because I just showed her my cards and now she knows how I really feel about her. I'm doing my very best not to let on how petrified I am when she closes her mouth with a, "Haha!"

"What?" I ask.

She shakes her head with a knowing glare. "That's like, eighty percent of women. I bet you got that from reading a magazine O2 left at your place."

I can't tell if she really believes that or if she only wants to believe it because it makes her feel better. But, for right now, I'm not going to push it. I've already said enough about both of our sex lives for one evening and I don't want to push her away.

"I'm sure I did," I say. "Because we all know how much I love reading women's magazines. Maybe I know it because I read those romance novels you have hanging all over your place when I come by to take you somewhere and I have to wait for you to get ready. Or maybe it's from watching all those kissing movies you always seem to pick out for us to watch."

"You are so full of it." She shakes her head.

I know I am, but it's all I could think of to say to somehow keep her from guessing the truth.

"A," she says. "You never have to wait for me because I'm always ready to go long before you show up. B, I don't read print books. That's what my e-reader is for. And C, if I remember correctly, I said you weren't allowed to watch any romance movies with me because you spent most of your time yelling at the hero to grow a pair and be a man."

I snap. "That's right. I forgot."

She tilts her head and looks at me as if she's trying to

figure out what in the world is wrong with me. I don't care one bit because it means she's no longer thinking about how I know what she likes in bed.

We both drop it then, allowing some of the tension to leave the table. In fact, we don't talk about anything having to do with relationships until we're finishing dessert.

"Like I said earlier, you really should let me set you up with someone."

I roll my eyes. "Really Darc? Back to that? You really think you can find someone for me better than I can find myself?"

"I'm sure of it," she says and then pops the last bite of her double mocha cake in her mouth.

I almost tell her she's on just so it'll hopefully wipe that smirky grin off her face before I'm tempted to kiss it off. "That's okay," I say instead, not able to drag my gaze from her lips. "I'll pass."

But it appears as if in remembering everything about how Darcy likes sex, I forgot one thing: she likes to play dirty. Therefore, I'm not at all prepared when her grin goes from smirky to downright evil.

"Come on," she says, proving once and for all how well she does know me because the next three words are my own personal kryptonite. "I dare you."

CHAPTER THREE: DARCY

"THE ONLY THING WORSE THAN A BOY
WHO HATES YOU: A BOY THAT LOVES YOU."
MARKUS ZUSAK

*I*t's a prick move on my part. Before the words even leave my mouth, I know I'm stooping low.

Across the table, he's looking at me and not once does his gaze waver. "You're playing with fire, Darc."

Darc. There he goes with the nickname again. Honestly, I don't know what has gotten into him. It's been months since he last used it. Talk about fire, that nickname combined with his heat in his eyes is close to setting me aflame. The entire evening with him has been one surprise after another. From him showing up alone, to the admission about O2. The sex talk about what he likes. Not to mention, his long discourse on what he believes I want from a man in bed.

I will not think about how right he was or try to figure out how he knows.

"Why?" I ask him. "You can't honestly think I can do worse than you. Seriously, let's take a few minutes to look over your last few dates. Or, wait...what do you call a person like O2? I'm not sure date fits? Maybe the 'scratcher of my libido itch'?"

No answer from him. He continues to stare at me with *that* gaze.

Finally, he speaks, but his voice is much coarser than normal. "You know I can't turn down a dare," he says. "Instead of getting mad at you for using that against me, I'll make you a deal."

"What kind of a deal?" Normally I would never bother asking, because *normally* no matter what deal he came up with it would benefit us both. But tonight, I'm not so sure. Not now. Not with this new, definitely not normal, Elliott that I can't quite grasp and has nearly upended my world.

I try very hard not to fidget as I wait for him to answer my question.

"I agree to take you up on the dare," he says. "But in return, *I* dare *you* to let me set you up."

"We get to set each other up?" I ask. "Will we double date, too?"

"No," he's quick to answer. "I don't think that would be a good idea. You and I would probably spend the entire time talking to each other."

I laugh because I can totally see that happening. Elliott gives me a big smile, and for this one moment, we're back to where we've always been. The only problem is, I don't know if that's what I want.

LATER, after we say our goodbyes, when I'm back at my house alone, in bed, and not able to go to sleep, I give myself the freedom to think. I can't lie and say I have never thought about Elliott *that* way before, in a sexual way. Seriously, he is a fine looking man with a fine looking body, and he knows how to use it. But earlier tonight, when he asked those questions about his preferences, I had a strange feeling he wasn't talking about a date. I think he was talking about me.

No matter how many times I might have fantasized about Elliott that way, it had never been as vivid as it had been while listening to him vocalize it. Even now, as I let a hand drift between my legs, I hear him whispering that he'll take my pussy any way I give it to him. And though I'm sure he meant it hypothetically, I close my eyes and it's the realest thing I've ever felt.

I've held his hand before, I know what his fingers feel like and it doesn't take much to imagine them sliding up my thighs and his hands parting them so he can slide between. I don't know how he tastes, but I know the feel of his lips and just the thought of those lips nibbling along my inner thigh is nearly enough to send me over the edge. But I hold out until I'm almost positive I can feel his warm breath teasing about how wet I am for him. His growl of masculine approval at how much he turns me on is music to my ears as he makes good on his promise about his tongue.

I pant as I picture his head between my legs, his lips on my folds, and his tongue licking me where I've never before pictured him. The feeling is so good, so intense, I force myself not to come because I don't want it to end. In my mind, he slowly crawls up my body. I pinch my nipples with my other hand pretending they are Elliott's fingers and I almost come again.

But I won't let myself. Not until I picture him above me, looking intent as he lines himself up. I image what he feels like slowly entering me, stretching me, giving me his entire length, and in my mind he's large, long, and thick.

He whispers he's waited too long, and he has to fuck me hard. I can only nod before he pulls out only to thrust back inside and sinking even deeper. He calls out my name in a way and with an urgency he's never used with me before. And through it all I'm working just as hard as he is, lifting up to meet him thrust for thrust, and I realize I'm chanting his name.

"Elliott. Yes. Harder."

He answers, my dream Elliott, giving me exactly what I want until we both release together.

After my climax passes, I wait for an icky feeling to come over me. It should, shouldn't it? He's my closest friend, and even though I think that should make him feel like a brother, it doesn't. Instead he feels exactly like what he is—a guy I've been friends with forever, who also happens to be hot as hell.

It doesn't make me strange or a pervert. It makes me a normal female. The fact that hearing him talk about the way he'd pleasure me was a turn on? Again, normal female reaction. Getting aroused as he described the various ways he might use me if I went to my knees in front of him? Seriously? What other reaction could I possibly have?

This does not mean, however, that I will ever tell him any of this. Not that hearing him talk about sex turned me on and definitely not that I got myself off while thinking about him.

Hell to the no, underline, bold, and extra exclamation points.

Because as soon as Elliott sees me as someone other than his best friend, that's when I'll become whatever thing he sees. I can't stand the thought of not being his best friend anymore. Lovers came and went. Heck, I'd personally seen Elliott with at least two different women each month. They were nothing to him. Likewise, he was nothing to them.

But I'm not like O2, nor do I want to be. As wonderful and mind-blowing as I'm sure it is to be in his bed, I'd never exchange that for our friendship. Elliott has been the one constant in my life that has never left me. My parents divorced when I was eleven. My dad died five years ago. Only Elliott has been my steady support through it all.

So if I had to pick between sex with Elliott and Elliott my friend, friend Elliott wins every time. I can give myself orgasms. I can't give myself a new Elliott.

However, for the first time ever, I feel as if friend Elliott is missing something.

CHAPTER FOUR: ELLIOTT

"GOD GAVE MEN BOTH A PENIS AND A BRAIN, BUT UNFORTUNATELY NOT ENOUGH BLOOD SUPPLY TO RUN BOTH AT THE SAME TIME." ROBIN WILLIAMS

I arrive at work the next day at an ungodly early hour to our downtown office. The admin looks up in surprise when I walk in, but I only nod and continue toward the back where I work during the off season. Before heading to my office, I stop in the break room and make the strongest pot of coffee I can both stand and get away with.

I realized the deep shit I was in once I got home the night before. I'm still running on much too little sleep, but with help from the obnoxiously strong coffee, I feel certain I'm making the right decision.

When I agreed to Darcy's ridiculous dare last night and made the condition that I would also pick a date for her, I'll admit, my initial plan had been to get back at her. Don't get me wrong, I would never set her up with a jerk or anyone who would be less than respectful. But a self-absorbed jock who could only talk about himself? Yes, and that would serve her right for suggesting the dare in the first place.

But I can't do that to her.

I take a sip of the coffee and burn the roof of my mouth, but it doesn't distract me from my main goal. I pull out the box

23

of business cards I've collected over the years and look for the one belonging to one of the few men I'm acquainted with who is good enough for Darcy. I half hope I can't find it and will have to fall back on my plan of egotistical athlete, but within seconds my fingers wrap around the innocent cardstock that will both bring my damnation and serve as my salvation.

Tate Maddox.

Most people won't recognize the name and that's okay because that's what Tate wanted when he left the world of professional sports behind as well as the name everyone does know—Tommy Maddox. After a wildly successful five years in baseball, Tommy did the unthinkable and walked away from everything, claiming he didn't like what fame was making him into and stating he didn't need any more money.

Yes, he actually said that.

Now he runs a sports camp for underprivileged children. It's the exact kind of thing Darcy loves and I can see her getting into. I can use one hand to count the number of guys I think might be worthy of her. Tate is the only one who is her age and also single.

I tell myself I'm doing the right thing. If I can't have her, I need her to be with someone who will respect her and love her for who she is. Who can appreciate the woman underneath the gorgeous exterior.

It's probably the most painful thing I've ever done, but I dial his number. I close my eyes as his phone rings and even though it's probably wrong, I hope against hope that he won't answer.

Someone picks up on the fourth ring and my heart sinks.

"Hello?" they answer.

It's him. I recognize his voice. I put on a happy face and think maybe since we're not in the same room he won't be able to tell it's fake. "Tate?"

"Yes."

"It's Elliott Taber."

He pauses for a minute, I assume he's trying to place me. "Trainer for The Storm," he finally remembers. "Yes. How are you?" His voice is hesitant, not that I can blame him. I would be, too if I was in his place.

"Great," I say. "But I'm not actually calling for anything professional or sports related. It's a personal thing." He's silent so I continue, "I'm not sure if you've ever met my friend Darcy Patrick? Anyway, the other night she dared me to let her set me up with someone she picked and I agreed only if I could do the same and pick someone for her."

"Okay," he says, and I'm not sure I even want to know what he's thinking at the moment.

All I can do is hope he doesn't hang up on me. "The thing is she's more than a friend. She's my best friend. I've known her for almost my entire life." I force myself to take a deep breath. "I guess it's safe to say I have strong opinions about the kind of man I feel is good enough for her. And I'd like to know if you're still single and if so, if you're interested?"

He's quiet for so long I fear we've been disconnected but then I hear him exhale. He better not ask me to repeat any of that because it was pure luck I got it out the first time. I don't have it in me to say it a second time.

"Has she ever gone with you to a Storm event?"

"Yes. She's typically the only person I take. Especially the last few years."

I can hear his frown over the phone. "But you're not together. You're just friends?"

"Right." I ball my free hand into a fist and then relax it once more.

"I'm pretty sure I know who she is. I believe we were introduced once. And you think she'll be okay with you setting her with me?"

"Yes. She follows baseball. She knows who you are, I'm sure. She'll more than likely be beside herself." That much I know is true. I hate it, but it's the truth.

"And you two aren't together or anything? Because from what I remember you two looked pretty tight."

"Me and Darcy? No way, man. I don't think of her that way." It's the most hideous lie I've ever told and it would be totally justified for lightning to strike me dead for saying something so blasphemous.

My chest hurts at the magnitude of the untruth I spoke. There's nothing to do other than to finish this.

"Yes, of course," he says. "I'm honored you think so highly of me and I'd love to take Darcy out. Do I call her or, how are you guys working this?"

He sounds way too excited and eager for my peace of mind but it's too late to renege my offer.

I clear my throat. "I'll give you her number, but do me a favor and don't call her until tomorrow. I want to give her a head's up." Actually, what I want to do is to give her a chance to call this whole thing off, but he doesn't need to know that.

He agrees. Of course he fucking does. Who wouldn't? We say our goodbyes and for several long minutes, I stare at my phone.

Finally, unable to put off the inevitable, I call Darcy and of course, she picks up on the first ring. Of course she does.

"Hey, Elliott," she almost sings.

"Someone must have gotten some sleep last night," I tease back, even as the sound of her voice makes me smile. I'm a bit surprised. After that phone call with Tate, I felt I might never smile again. Regardless, Darcy sounds rested. I'm glad one us was able to sleep. It for damn sure wasn't me.

"Not really," she says. "But I'm sitting here thinking about you and trying to decide who would be the best person to set you up with."

She's so excited about this and I tell myself I'll act the same, even if it kills me. Which it could possibly do. Has anyone actually died of a broken heart?

"Funny," I say. "I was just doing the same. However, I've already decided who your perfect match is and called him. He'll be in touch with you tomorrow."

"Wow. That was quick."

I drop my voice. "There are only a handful of men I think worthy of you, Darc."

"That's so sweet of you," she says, and I know her cheeks are now that delicate pink shade they get when she's embarrassed. I want to know more than the color though, I want to touch the pink and feel the heat radiate from her skin.

"It's the truth," I tell her, making myself forget about touching her. I forge ahead to get the rest out before all the lies and untruths I've spoken over the last hour make me mute. "You've actually met this guy before. Though I didn't remember until he mentioned being introduced to you."

"I know him?" She asks with unmasked excitement.

"Yes," I say, and even though I love to tease her, I'm not going to about this. "Tate Maddox. He used to go by the name Tommy Maddox."

"Oh, my God," she says, and I know she is aware of exactly who he is. "That's the guy who walked away from that huge contract because he said all the money in the world wasn't worth losing his soul over."

"Yes."

She squeals. Fucking squeals.

For the record, Darcy has never squealed. Ever. I hold the phone away from my ear in shock. When I put it back in place so I can hear what she's saying, I rather wish I hadn't because her words almost rip my heart apart.

"Oh my God," she repeats. "I was so floored by him and what he said and that he actually followed through. Do you know how rare that is? What does he do now? And I really met him once? When was it? How is it I don't remember and he does? What did he say about me? Tell me, Elliott. Tell me every single word of your conversation and don't leave anything out."

Fuck my life.

CHAPTER FIVE: DARCY

"DON'T LOOK FOR A PARTNER WHO IS EYE
CANDY. LOOK FOR A PARTNER WHO IS
SOUL FOOD." KAREN SALMANSOHN

I end my phone call with Elliott while wearing a
stupid grin. I'm still in shock he's set me up with
Tommy—*Tate*—I correct myself, Maddox. It never even
occurred to me he could possibly be someone Elliott might
pick. Not because I'm not interested, but because Tate has
been out of the spotlight for so long. I hate to admit it, but to
be honest, I forgot about him until Elliott brought him up.

I search 'Tate Maddox' from my computer at work and
wonder how he's changed since I last saw his picture. Most
of what populates my screen are old news stories from when
he turned down the eight figure contract New York offered
him. I skip over those, hoping to find something · more
recent, but I take a few seconds to appreciate the images my
search returns.

The Golden Son, the news outlets delighted in calling
him and even now as I look over the pictures from years ago,
it's easy to see why. The images highlight his all natural
good looks—his sun-kissed hair and deep blue eyes, paired
with a heartwarming smile showing perfect white teeth.
Wrap that together with the way he can hit a ball and how

he always says 'ma'am' and 'sir', and you have every woman's dream date who is also the dream son-in-law of both her mother and father.

I'm not able to find anything recent, however, so I filter the results to only show items from the last year. Even then, almost everything references back to the past. Finally, on the bottom of the fourth page, from a website I've never heard of, is a "Where Are They Now?" article that gives him three paragraphs of text.

I'm floored by what I read. He currently lives in the Blue Ridge Mountains where he has built and oversees a year-round camp dedicated to improving the lives of underprivileged children. I wonder if Elliott knows this, but of course he does. The article states Tate is still in contact with numerous sports programs and that the camp is an organization many of those programs support.

In fact, didn't Elliott say I had met Tate at one of the charity balls I went with him to or did he only say 'an event'? And why the hell do I not remember this at all?

Without thinking about it too much, I send Elliott a text.

Did I meet Tate at a charity ball?

His reply is quick.

IDK, he just said an event.

That doesn't help me at all.

Why don't I remember?

Maybe you were drunk.

I rarely get drunk.

It's the truth and he knows it. Our high school senior trip had been to the Bahamas and the drinking age was eighteen. We partook a bit too freely and later on we were both too sick to enjoy most of the trip.

My guess is you didn't recognize him when introduced as Tate.

I stare at his text for a long time, thinking back to the last few black ties I went to with Elliott and searching my brain for when I possibly met Tate. Unfortunately, I come up with nothing.

I text Elliott back.

I guess you're right. Makes me feel bad.

His reply is almost instant.

Don't worry about it. I didn't remember it either.

I send him a heart, knowing that even if he did, he would say he didn't so I wouldn't feel bad.

I'm not expecting a response, so when my phone buzzes a minute later, I look at it in shock. But after reading what he sent, I laugh.

You're welcome, by the way. Also, I expect an equally as awesome date. :P

I have to admit he's raised the bar considerably. Before discovering who he selected for me, I had planned on a woman from my yoga class, but now I'm not sure. She's nice and attractive, but she is nowhere near as great of a date as Tate is. I could probably work myself into a panic if I think about it enough. After all, the entire date thing was my idea and I did tell Elliott that I know him better than he knows himself. Because of that, I have to ensure the partner I pick for him blows his mind.

I text him back.

Just you wait...

He doesn't answer and after waiting a few minutes, I start scrolling through the contacts on my phone. Come hell or high water, I will find him the date to end all dates.

Ten minutes later, I admit she is not going to be found in my phone. Undeterred, I begin to look over my email lists. She's in here somewhere. She has to be. And I won't stop until either I find her or she finds me.

Someone knocks on my office door before I get too involved in my search. It's a good thing and even though I'm irritated, I need to put it away until after work. Reluctantly, I close my email and tell whoever is at the door to come in.

It's my boss, Meredith, but she's not alone. With her is a stunningly beautiful woman. She's tall with gorgeous red hair that is so fiery there's no way it's a bottle job. Her eyes are green and when she smiles, they light up her entire face.

"Darcy," Meredith says. "This is Kara Devine. She's going to be our spokeswoman for the new Asia-Pac sites. I thought since you'd been there recently, you could give her some inside information."

Normally, this is not my favorite thing to do. I have too much other stuff to get through. Meredith knows this and as she's been speaking, her eyes have been pleading with me.

I surprise her by saying, "Sure." I turn to Kara. "Do you have time now?"

Kara takes a backward glance at Meredith, who is obviously still shell-shocked that I didn't argue. "Of course," she says. "I'll be in my office when you finish," she tells Kara.

Meredith hurries out my door as if expecting me to call her back and tell her I've changed my mind. I don't, of course.

Instead what I do is wait until she closes the door and then turn to Kara. "So," I say to her. "Do you like lacrosse?"

CHAPTER SIX: ELLIOTT

"DATE SOMEONE BECAUSE YOU ALREADY
SEE A FUTURE, NOT BECAUSE YOU WANT
TO SEE IF YOU WOULD WORK OUT." SARAH
MOORES

A week after I set Darcy up with Tate, she calls me with the name of the woman she's selected for me. Kara Devine. Darcy says she's a local actress who is doing some marketing and promo for the hotel chain. She admits Kara isn't the woman she originally selected for me, but that she recently met Kara and after talking with her for the last week, she believes we'll be perfect together.

She's wrong, but I don't correct her. Let her think what she wants. Technically, I suppose, Kara could be my soulmate. There's also a chance little purple men will invade Atlanta, which I think is far more likely, but you don't see me preparing for battle.

Darcy tells me to call Kara today and confirm the date. For some reason, Darcy has in her mind that our dates should occur on the same day. I don't see the point, but I'll do it because it'll make her happy.

Before I make the call to Kara, I do a search of her name online and I'm pleasantly surprised by what I find. It's not that I thought Darcy would lie, it's just that sometimes she stretches the truth. The way she kept going on and on about how gorgeous Kara is actually had me thinking she was the exact opposite.

I'm typically not a big fan of red hair, but as I look at the pictures of Kara online, I realize it's probably because I've never gone out with a natural redhead before. Kara's eyes are also captivating. A deep green that pulls my attention. Granted, there is no way she will ever take the place of Darcy either in my life or my fantasies. But to hang around with? It might actually be fun to go on more than one date with a woman.

I'm actually feeling a little excited as I punch her number into my phone.

Later, I'm meeting Darcy for dinner. It's the first time we've been able to get together since she proposed this plan. I'm not bringing anyone with me this time either, and if it's odd I'm more excited about this dinner than the upcoming date with Kara, I don't even care. As per always, she's beaten me to the restaurant and is practically jumping up and down in the booth when she sees me. It's a casual bistro so no one bats an eye when she waves me over to sit with her.

"Elliott!"

It's like whenever I'm around her I can't stop smiling. I can't help it.

"Hey, Darc." I lean over and kiss her cheek before sliding in across from her. I can't remember when I started kissing her, but now I never leave without brushing my lips across the smooth skin of her cheek. I'm not sure it's body wash, shampoo, or something else, but that scent reminds me of the summers we spent together as children.

"Kara said you called her," she says by way of greeting.

"Did you doubt me when I said I would?" I arch an eyebrow.

"No. I just didn't think you'd do it that quickly."

I decide not to go down that road any further. I hadn't planned to call her so quickly. For some completely illogical reason it felt like the whole deal wouldn't be real until I spoke with Kara.

"She seems really nice," I tell Darcy, hoping that will steer her away from why I called her so quickly.

Because Darcy doesn't need to know how ready I am to get this whole thing over and done with.

"She really is," Darcy says and I can't remember what I said about Kara. "A lot of the time, or if I'm being honest, most of the time, people with a job like hers are stuck up."

I haven't met a lot actresses, definitely not any who would be considered an A-lister, and Kara doesn't qualify for that list, either. The few I've met have mostly been dates of the men on the team. "Do you know a lot of actresses?"

"No, but remember when we had that guy who was nominated for an Academy Award and all that crap we had to set up just to get him to shoot a few commercials?"

I laugh. "The one who insisted on having three round ice cubes in his water, and only ate blue candy?"

"Yes." She rolls her eyes. "I swear to this day I can't eat a blue piece of candy."

"You're not going to tell me Kara's like that, are you? Should I start making ice balls and buying up all the blue candy I can find?" Surely Darcy knows better than to set me up with a diva.

"No," she's quick to reply. "Kara is nothing like him. Which is why I brought it up. She's so down to earth, I find it hard to believe she spends a lot of her time in front of the camera."

Her observation sparks a question. "Do you think pro athletes are a lot like actors?"

She tilts her head. "I think they can be. Especially some of the well known ones."

"Like what Tate might have turned into if he'd stayed Tommy?"

Her mouth forms an "O" of surprise. "Tell me you didn't set me up with a diva ex-ball player."

"Tate? No way. He's about as far from a diva as you can get. Remember, he left the game." It shocks me that she even thought I'd set her up with a diva athlete. Well, I did *think* about it, but I didn't go through with it. That's the important part.

"Okay," she says, clearly relieved. "That's what I thought, I just wanted to make sure."

"Let's not forget this whole date thing was your idea," I tell her. "I think I've set you up with a really great guy, especially since I didn't have much time to think about it."

It strikes me that maybe I should have thought about it for at least a little bit longer. Looking back, I set her up with more that a great guy. I set her up with the perfect guy.

"Are you okay?" she asks with a lift of her eyebrow. "You don't look like you feel good all of a sudden."

I cough to cover both my expression and to stop myself from blurting out the truth. "Yes. I'm fine. Just remembered something I need to do for a meeting tomorrow."

But even though I try to cover it up, the question won't stop repeating in my head:

What the hell have I done?

CHAPTER SEVEN: DARCY

"LOVE IS WHEN THE OTHER PERSON'S
HAPPINESS IS MORE IMPORTANT THAN
YOUR OWN." H. JACKSON BROWN, JR

*T*ate is early to pick me up for our date and that, of
course, endears him to me even more. Namely,
because I'm always early no matter where I'm going, but
also because in this case, I've been ready for half an hour.

He isn't able to hide his surprise when he sees I'm
ready. "I'm usually not this early," he says as I try to usher
him inside, but he doesn't take a step forward. Seeing my
confusion, he hastens to add, "I have a few things I need to
get out of my car. If you don't mind."

"Why would I mind?"

"Maybe I hang out with the wrong crowd, but you'd be
surprised," is all he says before he turns around and heads
back to his car.

"You're probably right," I say because I'm always
shocked by people. Especially the way they can treat other
people. Elliott says it's because I'm too nice and always try
to find the good in a situation or person.

My reply obviously isn't the one Tate was expecting
either. He glances over his shoulder and gives me a grin that
steals my breath and suddenly I remember the function

we'd both attended. It was the Holiday Charity Ball two years ago and Tate wasn't a guest. He was working the buffet line with who I now know were some of the older kids he works with.

I'm shocked and humbled by that fact. Not to mention, a bit embarrassed. My fingers itch to call Elliott and tell him, but his date with Kara started over an hour ago.

"Anything I can help you with?" I manage to ask Tate, pushing everything else out of my mind for now.

"Sure," he says, and I walk with him toward his car, but follow a few steps behind so I can take a good look at him. He still matches my definition of the Golden Son with his sun-kissed, tousled hair and blue eyes. It's his demeanor that has changed the most. There's a settled calmness about him that indicates he is at peace with himself, the world, and his place in it. It's not something I see very often and it's definitely a turn on.

We make it to his car and he unlocks the doors. He opens the back one, revealing piles of grocery bags. So many.

"Are you planning to feed an army?" I tease.

"Something like that." He hands me a few bags and I'm surprised at how light they are. I peek inside and all I see are loaves of bread.

"Are you sure you're okay with me bringing all of this inside?" he asks again.

"I don't mind at all," I tell him. "In fact, you might win the award for Most Intriguing Way to Start a First Date Ever."

He laughs at that, a deep and rich sound that makes me smile, and follows me inside. I live in a two-bedroom townhouse. It's really too much space since I live by myself and travel so frequently. But I love it. It's the first place I ever bought and it was ridiculously cheap when I found it because the previous owners had to sell quickly due to an unexpected relocation. I could sell it and make a nice profit, but I can't talk myself into it.

Tate follows me into the kitchen. I'm very curious about what he has in the bags he's carrying and why in the world he's bought so much bread. He places his bags on the island. We've talked several times, on the phone and via text, but he's never given a hint about what he has planned for tonight. The only thing he would tell me is that I should dress casual for the first part.

I've never been on a date with parts and I can't lie about how excited I am. Tate is dressed similarly to me, wearing jeans and a tee-shirt. He looks right at home in my kitchen, unpacking the grocery bags. He takes out a few jars of peanut butter and a few more of jelly, and finally a box of disposable sandwich bags.

"It's not a very common first date activity," he says. "But I know from talking with you that you hold many of the same values and beliefs I do. So I thought we should make and deliver peanut butter and jelly sandwiches to the homeless downtown. Are you good with that?"

It's like nothing I've ever done, first date or not, and it sounds wonderful. One of those things I've always think about doing, but never get around to actually doing. Usually, the thought will hit me as I'm walking downtown or somewhere similar. You know, I'm already there and probably on my way to somewhere else or to do something else. Bottom line is, I never think about it when it's actually a good time to do something, though I'm shamed to admit it.

"I love that idea," I tell Tate, and tension I hadn't even noticed him having, leaves his shoulders.

"I'm so glad you're excited about it," he says with a

tentative smile. "I was afraid you wouldn't like the idea, and I'd be stuck with a ton of peanut butter, jelly, and bread. I wouldn't know what to do with it all."

"No way." I wonder about the women he's been dating if that's the case. "How could anyone not get excited and not want to do something like this?"

"You'd be surprised about what I've heard in the past," he says. "Remember what I told you outside a few minutes ago, right before I went to get the bags from my car?"

"That you've been hanging with the wrong crowd."

"It certainly does seem that way, doesn't it?"

We stand in silence for a few seconds. The late afternoon air humming around us. I'm struck again by just how perfect he looks and now it appears as if his personality is the same. He watches me so intently, it's almost as if he's studying me. I'm fully aware that even on my best days I'm nowhere near the person Tate is.

"What are you thinking?" he asks.

I get out a few butter knives so we can start on the sandwiches. "If you must know, I'm thinking two things. One, do you have any flaws? I'll even take a minor one, like do you have toothpaste spatters on your bathroom mirror? And two, I'm too much of a bitch to ever consider going out with you."

He steps toward me and takes a knife from my hand. "One, yes, I have plenty of flaws and the more you're around me, the more you'll see them and yes, I do have toothpaste spatters on my bathroom mirror. As for your last statement, I don't believe there is anything bitchy about you, and if it's okay, I'll be the one to determine who I go out with, and for tonight it's you."

I'm speechless. There are absolutely no words in my brain to even try to think of a response to him. But a quick glance to the island shows he's not waiting for one. He's already setting up an assembly line so we can start on the sandwiches.

"How about if I get the bread out and spread the peanut butter and you take care of the jelly and putting them in a bag. When all the bread is gone, together we make sure the bags are sealed and pack them all into the grocery bags?"

I nod, still believing I'm not a nice enough person for him. But he looks pretty set on going through with this date. The way I see it, he's been warned. However, at the moment, I don't feel bitchy at all. I'm both happy and excited to see how this date goes.

I get into my position near the jelly and bags. "Hurry up with the bread and peanut butter up there," I tease. "We don't have all night, you know."

He laughs. "Don't rush me. There's an art to spreading this stuff. You don't want an incorrectly spread peanut butter on your conscience, do you?"

I hold my hand up to my throat as if that's the most shocking thing I've ever heard. "Heavens, no. Whatever would we do then? What would the neighbors say? What if the peanut butter company found out? They might prohibit us from ever buying peanut butter again and then what would happen?"

With all seriousness, Tate looks at me and replies, "Then there would be no way for us to make PB&Js. We'd have to only make Js and no one knows what those are."

I shake my head and match my tone of voice to his. "We definitely can't have that. Forget what I said earlier. Take as long as you need on the peanut butter."

He laughs and I feel better about tonight. He grabs a few slices of bread and my phone rings as I'm waiting for him to pass me the first sandwich. I glance at the display and frown.

Tate waves at me. "Go on and answer it," he says, catching my expression. "I've got this."

"It's okay." I turn the phone off and slide it into my pocket, but I can't hide my frown. "It's Elliott, but he's out with a friend of mine. Probably a butt dial."

"Are you sure you don't need to call him, just in case?"

There's no way I'm talking to Elliott now because I'd blurt out how we met Tate before and that wouldn't be the best thing to do with Tate standing three feet from me.

"I'm positive. Let's make some sandwiches."

CHAPTER EIGHT: ELLIOTT

"YOU NEVER RUN OUT OF THINGS THAT
CAN GO WRONG." EDWARD A. MURPHY

*M*y call rolls over to Darcy's voicemail, and I hang up with a curse. Tate Fucking Maddox. A look at my watch tells me that her date with the man has started. Just like mine was supposed to, almost an hour and half ago. I'm not sure what the problem is. I've already placed several phone calls to Kara. But none of them have been answered. I can't believe she's going to be a no-show, especially after all the things Darcy has said about her. But it appears as if for once that Darcy is wrong.

I have to admit, I'm surprised. I never heard any sort of hesitation on the phone with Kara. In fact, she's always seemed very happy about the things I have planned to do today. Another look at my watch tells me that there's no way we could be on time for kickoff, even if we were to leave right now.

I wonder if this why she didn't want me to pick her up at her house and why she insisted on meeting here, at the food court of a local mall. I dial Darcy's number again. If she's ignoring me, maybe if I call enough she'll have pity on me.

I feel like an idiot and I'm pretty sure I look like one as well. For the life of me, I'm not sure why I'm still waiting here when my date is over an hour late. On second thought, yes I do. As soon as I leave, I'll be admitting I got stood up. It shouldn't bother me, I don't even want this date.

Fucking hell. I slip my sunglasses on and head to the door. Before I can reach it, it opens and a stunning redhead enters. She glances around, obviously looking for someone. Her gaze lands on me and her face lights up. I must have 'Fuck Off' stamped on my forehead, because her expression dims just as quickly.

"Elliott?" she asks.

There's no way this woman is Kara. Not breezing in here like nothing's wrong when she's an hour and a half late.

"Yes," I say, and then because there is no other viable explanation, ask, "Kara?"

She nods. "Are you leaving?"

I'm telling myself to hold it together and not jump to conclusions because she does look a bit confused. Maybe she has some sort of disorder or something. "I was," I admit. "I've been waiting an hour and a half."

"Why have you been here that long?" She looks at her watch. "I'm early as it is."

I'm trying to see how she thinks this. "What?"

"Oh no," she says. "The game *starts* in twenty minutes, doesn't it?"

"Yes."

She closes her eyes. "I am so sorry. I thought we were meeting then and that the game started later. That certainly explains why the attendant at the gas station looked at me funny." She shakes her head. "You should have called me."

Is she serious? "I did," I tell her. "Multiple times."

44

She digs in her purse and pulls out her phone. "No missed calls." She turns it to face me and sure enough the screen is blank.

I pull out my own phone to prove to myself I'm not making this up. There in my history are the calls I made to her. I hold the phone out. She gasps and covers her mouth with her hand.

"That's my landline, not my cell." She looks horrified as she realizes everything. "I'm so sorry."

It's a mixup, I repeat to keep myself calm. They happen all the time and I bet in the distant future, Darcy and I will laugh ourselves silly over this one. But it's not happening today. "It's okay," I tell Kara. "Mistakes happen."

"Though usually not so many at one time."

"True." But no need to dwell on it. I hold out my hand. "Elliott Taber. So good to finally meet you. Darcy speaks very highly of you."

She returns the handshake and I'm pleasantly surprised to discover her grip is strong. "I could say the same for you." She has a beautiful smile and I'm looking forward to seeing more of it tonight.

"What do you think, Kara?" I ask her. "Should we try to make it to the game? We'll probably be able to see the second half."

"I'd like that," she says. "Can you believe I've lived here my entire life and haven't made it to one professional game?"

I lift an eyebrow. "Of football?"

She shakes her head. "No, not of anything."

I suppose it's because I'm so heavily involved in sports that I find this hard to believe. "Baseball?" I ask, and she shakes her head. I try with several other sports, but she only laughs and repeats, "No."

45

Darcy asked if she enjoyed sports and Kara admitted to both watching and playing several. Interesting that she's never been to a pro game, especially with Atlanta having so many teams.

I smile because it's going to be fun watching her expression as she takes everything in for the first time. It's a shame she messed the time up because I'd have enjoyed showing her around the stadium before kickoff. I calculate when our dinner reservations are to see if we could explore after the game, but unfortunately, I don't think we'll have time.

I open my car door for her and we head out in the nightmare on wheels known as Atlanta traffic. The drive to the stadium isn't unpleasant. I ask Kara a few questions about her work, and she's enthusiastic in her responses and also asks me several things about what I do.

We have a nice chat.

Kara is a nice woman.

It's boring as hell.

It's not that I want a bad girl. It's not that I don't like to talk about my job. It's that I want so much more than to be in a nice relationship with a nice woman and to have a nice life. I want fire and passion and heated debates and being there for someone no matter what.

I don't doubt that I could settle down with Kara. I would probably be mostly happy. I would do everything in my power to make her happy. But at the end of the day, it wouldn't be the right thing to do because my heart wouldn't be hers. It wouldn't be fair to Kara. She can't help that she isn't Darcy.

We're almost to the stadium and I tell myself I'm an idiot for thinking the way I am about a woman I just met.

Seriously, what does it say that I've already mapped our entire future, other than I'm an idiot?

Beside me, Kara is talking animatedly about her older brother, who lives in North Carolina and recently took his son to a football game there.

"He's going to be so jealous when I tell him about this," she says, her smile growing bigger the closer we get.

Likewise, I start to feel calmer as we approach our destination. I'm allowed to have a fun date with a nice woman. It doesn't mean I have to marry her. We'll spend a pleasant afternoon together and have a delicious dinner and call it a night. I may call her again, but probably not.

I park and help Kara out of the car. We make our way to the entrance closest to where our seats are. As we walk, I tell her a few little known facts about the stadium.

It feels as if the date that had started out so badly is redeeming itself when the man working the gate looks at me and says, "I can't let you in with these tickets, sir."

CHAPTER NINE: DARCY

"A MAN'S TRUE WEALTH IS THE GOOD HE
DOES IN THIS WORLD." MUHAMMAD

*W*e are only about a quarter of the way through passing out the sandwiches when I get that crawly neck feeling that I'm being watched. I try to ignore it and when that doesn't work, I tell myself it's because I'm with Tate and he's so hot or it's because of the fact we're the only ones passing out food.

We stop to drink some of the bottled water Tate has stashed in his car and that's when a young woman who looks like she might be in college approaches us.

"I support what you're doing," she says. "But you should know, I got a ticket for doing the same thing last week. You might want to stay away from the police."

I'm not sure I've ever heard anything so stupid in my life. "Are you serious? You got a ticket for giving food to people who don't have any?" I'm not sure what it says about our city that they would make such a law. It seems so cold and harsh. I look over to Tate, but he doesn't seem shocked at all.

He catches me looking. "It's an old law and it's been on the books forever. They just never enforced it before. I didn't know they started." He thanks the young woman and she walks away. He turns to me. "Want to leave?"

"Are you kidding? No way." I throw my empty bottle away, ready to pass out more sandwiches. "I only wish we had more to give out."

"I knew I made the right decision," he says, taking a step toward me and for some reason, I feel like taking one back. I don't, but I'm shocked at my reaction to him moving in on my personal space. It's not like me. If I knew it wouldn't make me look as if I had a few screws loose, I'd smack myself. Because honestly, what's my problem?

Fortunately, Tate isn't picking up on my inner turmoil, but he doesn't move any closer either. "Shall we go break a few laws?" he asks, lifting an eyebrow and flashing me a grin.

I pat the sandwiches left in my bag. "Only the ones that need breaking and shouldn't have been made in the first place."

We're down to out last dozen or so sandwiches when I notice the cop watching us.

"Trouble. Three o'clock." My head is down so the cop doesn't see or hear me.

Tate sighs. "And to think we'd almost made it."

"What are you going to do?" I don't mind getting a ticket. In fact, part of me would love to get one just so I could show up in court and make a statement or something about how stupid this law is. However, I have no desire to do anything that might land me in jail. That is not how I want this date to end. "You aren't going to do anything to get arrested are you?" I ask him, keeping an eye on the uniformed man now headed our way.

"I certainly don't plan to." He lifts his head and faces the officer. "Good afternoon, sir. Would you like a sandwich? Just a little way for me to show my thanks for all you do to help keep Atlanta safe for all her citizens."

"Thank you, but no." He frowns. "I don't want a sandwich and I'm afraid I'm going to have to ask you and your lady friend here to stop handing them out."

The police officer is an older man and on the big side, probably not far from retirement. I'm sure he has a partner somewhere, but at the moment, I only see him.

"Is there a problem with us handing out sandwiches?" Tate asks. "You'll have to excuse me for not knowing. I'm only in town for the day, I'm from up near Tallulah Falls."

"You have to have a permit to hand out food to the homeless." The officer crosses his arms. "Handing out food is not a long-term solution. All it does is create a mess the city has to deal with."

Tate nods and looks quizzical as if he's taking all this in. "I guess that makes sense if you look at it that way."

The officer swells in victory. "I thought so, too. You two move along then."

I get the feeling he's not moving until we do. And Tate isn't about to walk away.

Sure enough, Tate taps his chin. "There's only one thing wrong with the city's long-term plan."

"What's that?"

"These people are hungry today." His voice is determined and I admire how he stands up for his beliefs.

"That's what the shelters are for."

The police officer may think he's won, but Tate has a look in his eye that says he isn't about to give up.

"I tell you what," Tate adds, and I can't help but notice their discussion is starting to draw a crowd. At the moment it's hard to know if this is a good thing or not. "If you can guarantee me that the people we haven't given a sandwich to yet will eat something tonight, my lady friend and I will leave."

The crowd around us murmurs in what I hope is approval.

"But if you can't." Tate shakes his head. "Don't ask me to turn my back and walk away. Not when I have in my hand something that could sustain them a little while longer."

There's the sound of gentle applause from behind me, and while Tate has the approval of our audience, the reddened face of the police officer tells us he doesn't feel the same. I have a bad feeling about this, and though everyone appears calm at the moment, I'm afraid it wouldn't take much for that to change.

Before the police officer can say anything, someone shouts, "You tell him, Tommy!" and the murmurs grow louder and people press closer. Tate doesn't say anything, but it's not too long until everyone realizes who he is. The officer knows eventually as well, but he's too good at his job to show any sort of amazement.

I'm a bit stunned there is so much excitement over Tate. I mean, it wasn't too long ago I could only find the vaguest of mentions of him online.

"Tommy Maddox?" the officer asks.

"Yes, sir," Tate replies. "But I don't expect any sort of preferential treatment. And I go by 'Tate' now."

"Well, Tate Maddox," he says, but before he can get anything else out, he's interrupted by a middle-aged woman wearing an apron.

"Officer Johnson, wait just a minute," she says, pushing through the crowd around us until she's at my elbow. She's a tiny thing. Based on her voice and how people move out of her way, I expect her to be taller than the barely five feet she appears.

"Maggie," Officer Johnson says in what sounds like a warning, but the tiny woman ignores him and faces Tate.

"My boy, Anderson, loved to watch you play. He always said you were the real deal."

"Thank you, ma'am." Tate is smiling, but it's an uneasy smile, and I can't help but to wonder if he's uncomfortable with all the attention.

"We lost him two years ago," Maggie continues. "In the Middle East. He was a Marine."

Tate's expression softens. "I'm sorry for your loss and, if I might say so, Anderson was the real deal."

Maggie nods, the slightest hint of tears in her eyes. "I'd hate for you and your date to get in any trouble when you're only trying to help." Maggie points to Officer Johnson. "Likewise, I'd hate for Officer Johnson to get into trouble when he's only trying to do his job." She leans forward and Tate and I do the same, expecting her to whisper. Instead, no one has trouble hearing her next words. "You know you don't necessarily have to agree with a law to enforce it."

"Maggie," Officer Johnson warns again.

Maggie waves at him. "Hush, you."

I glance at Officer Johnson just long enough to see him roll his eyes, but when he looks at her again, I can see he doesn't mind her at all. In fact, he looks a bit like a lovesick puppy. I catch Tate's eyes and clearly, he has seen it as well because he's grinning from ear to ear.

"As it turns out," Maggie says, and it's not my imagination that her cheeks are pinker than they were a few seconds ago. "I manage the soup kitchen right over there."

Tate and I look to where she's pointing. Not far from us is a large covered area with a line of people waiting to get in.

"If you'll hand me what you have left," Maggie says. "I'll ensure the sandwiches are given to some boys who will be thrilled to hear you made them."

"Thank you, ma'am." Tate gives her that show-stopping grin. "I truly appreciate you doing that."

"Of course," she continues as if he hadn't said anything. "It'd really make their day if you were to hand it to them yourself."

I giggle and try to hide it with a cough, but I'm pretty sure it doesn't work. I can't help it, though. I really like this Maggie.

Tate looks at me and lifts an eyebrow. I'm guessing he's asking if I mind stopping by the soup kitchen. If we do, there's a chance we could miss our dinner reservations. We both brought extra clothes to change into and time for that needs to be factored into our plans. The thing is, though, I'd rather watch Tate talk baseball with a group of young boys. I take his hand. "Let's go do it."

A few people in the crowd clap, but most of them start to leave. Maggie tells us to wait a minute and she'll walk us over. She takes Officer Johnson by the elbow and walks him a few steps away and out of hearing range.

The remaining crowd disperses and a handful of people pass by us to exchange a few words with Tate.

"Thank you," Tate says to me when the last of the crowd has left and Maggie's heading our way. I don't say anything, but I'm not sure why he's thanking me. I should be the one thanking him. Today is turning out to be completely unlike any date I've ever been on, but I'm enjoying it whole lot more as well.

I feel a bit odd as Tate and I walk into the food kitchen. Just because there are so many people who have no other way to eat tonight than to be right here, and not once have I ever had to worry about having enough food. It shames me I've never looked for ways to help before, and I vow to change. I'll even do it the legal way so I don't have to worry about unwelcome tickets. Tate appears to have no problem whatsoever and the ease with which he talks with everyone makes me feel even more awkward.

Maybe it's because he's a semi-celebrity or at least he once was. It would certainly explain why he's all smiles and handshakes and I'm like a tag along who decided to show up and follow him around.

I only have a minute or two of thinking those thoughts before Tate reaches for my hand, and pulls me into the conversation. Within seconds, those feelings slip away and yet, I still remember them because as the evening continues, there's a nagging feeling of something not being right.

We eventually sit down at a table with teenage boys who remember when Tate played ball. A small group of adults stand nearby as well, though they only want to listen as Tate recalls stories of past game days.

I sit back and try to see what it is about Tate that draws people to him. He's handsome enough, but there are other guys just as good looking. He's polite and kind, but there has to be more.

Someone brings us each a plate of food. I look around and catch the eye of Maggie. She's near the back, watching Tate interact with everyone, but I see her mouthed "thank you." I shrug and point to Tate, because really, it's all him. Then someone comes up to her and I get the feeling she's off to put out another fire.

As we're getting ready to leave, one of the teens from the table brings out an old baseball and shyly asks Tate if he'll sign it for his grandfather. He explains his grandfather is in the nearby VA hospital, and how much he loves baseball. Tate doesn't hesitate and goes a step further. After signing the ball, he asks me if I happen to have a notepad or other paper in my purse. I hand him the small notebook I keep handy, and he takes a sheet and writes a note for the young man to take as well.

That's when it hits me.

Tate's real. He's not fake and it shows. He's a genuinely nice guy and the realness radiates from him. I actually feel a little embarrassed I teased Elliott about setting me up with a diva because Tate is the exact opposite of a diva. Would that be an anti-diva? I wonder if that's even a word.

But more than that, I wonder if Elliott has set me up with a guy who is too perfect?

CHAPTER TEN: ELLIOTT

"FAILED RELATIONSHIPS CAN BE DESCRIBED AS SO MUCH WASTED MAKE-UP." MARIAN KEYES

*W*e end up at a sports bar nearby after three people at the stadium verify my tickets are fake. I'm fairly livid because I got them from a coworker who was unable to attend the game. I had assumed he was a season ticket holder, but he's not answering his phone.

"Don't worry about it." Kara puts her hand on my arm when I disconnect the call after getting his voicemail again.

She's no longer smiling, her eyes have lost their sparkle, and it's only a guess, but I'm pretty sure she won't be telling her brother about this after all. I can't help but think that if she had been on time, we might have been able to grab a few vacant seats. Of course, by the time we'd shown up, the game was in the second half and everything had been sold.

I put my phone down with a sigh. She's right. There's nothing to be done today. I'll deal with it on Monday. "I'm sorry," I tell her, because I feel responsible for the bad tickets.

"There's no way you could have known," she says, but her words don't make me feel better. I should have known. Somehow.

Neither one of us have been watching the game, but the bar is packed and suddenly everyone is chanting, clapping, and yelling. We both look up to the screen closest to us, just in time to watch an Atlanta player running down the field. No one is able to stop him and his touchdown wins the game.

Unfortunately, we don't notice the man standing near Kara forget he's holding a beer, and when he throws his hands up in victory, she is doused in his choice of brew.

IT'S NOT FUNNY, but I have to bite the inside of my cheek so I don't laugh. Kara is in the passenger seat beside me and even though she ducked into the bathroom at the sports bar, the inside of my car smells like a brewery.

She's asked for me to take her back to her car. I simply nodded because of course she doesn't want to go out to dinner smelling like a drunk and looking as if she's bathed in her favorite brew. I'm trying to remember if I've ever had a date go as badly as this one has, but I can't think of one. This has been, without question, the worst date I've ever been on. I'll make sure to thank Darcy tomorrow.

I exit off the interstate and wonder how Darcy's date with Tate is going. Surely there's no way it could possibly be as bad as this one. Granted, Kara's nice enough, but the two of us together seem doomed. Even now, she's sitting in the car, staring out the window and not saying anything. I should break the silence and say something, but I have no idea what to say.

I had a great time, obviously isn't going to work and based on her expression, I have a feeling that if I tell her I'd like to see her again, she might strike me dead with her eyes alone. I'm getting ready say to *At least no one ended up in the hospital or got arrested*, when I make a turn and see a police barricade straight ahead. I would laugh, but I have a bad feeling one of us is going to end up in jail before the night's over.

From all appearances, I think it's only a routine license check, but with the way this date has gone, you never know. I pull the car's registration and my driver's license, so I'm all prepared by the time I pull up to the uniformed man and roll my window down.

"Good evening, sir," I say, handing him the two documents.

He only looks at them briefly before turning his attention back to me. "Have you been drinking, Mr. Taber?"

I want to say a few choice words, because of course we smell like we've done nothing except drink for the last eight hours. "No, sir. We were watching the game at the Spotted Owl, though, and a man who had been drinking was standing next to us and when Atlanta made that last touchdown, forgot he was holding a beer and he inadvertently dumped it all over Kara here."

Kara turns her attention the officer, making sure he sees the drowned rat look she's rocking, but he only spares her a glance before he focuses back on me.

"Do you really expect me to believe you were at the Spotted Owl and didn't drink?"

"I didn't tell you that with hope you'd believe me. I said it because it's true."

He presses his lips together in a thin line, and though I hope he's getting ready to tell me to move on and have a great evening, I'm pretty sure that's not what's going to happen. Yet, I'm still in shock when he says, "I need you to pull over here to the side and step out of the car."

. . .

"Honestly, Darc," I say to her later that night when she calls to see how my date went. I've just given her a rundown of everything that happened and I don't have to see her to know she's trying her best not to laugh. "All I can say is, you are never allowed to set me up again."

"For the record," she says, swallowing her laughter. "I still think you and Kara would make a great couple."

"You're probably right." I think back to the thoughts I had earlier in the day about that same thing. "But I want to be with someone for a better reason than we'd make a great couple. I want to be with a woman who makes me great. Who makes me more than I am because of who we are together and someone that I make great as well."

I don't know. Maybe I said it wrong because Darcy isn't saying anything. Or maybe she's holding back, and what she really wants to ask is when I grew a vagina. But she doesn't do either.

Instead she sighs softly and whispers, "Yeah. I know what you mean."

"That doesn't make us crazy, does it? That we want more?"

"No, I don't think so." Her voice is small because she's thinking about what she wants to say. She rarely uses that tone so whatever she's going to say is very important to her. "Years ago, when I thought about the man I wanted to marry, I had a huge list of things I thought were important. Good job. Funny. That sort of thing. But the more and more I went out, I realized I already had a great guy as my best friend and whoever I ended up with not only had to measure up to you, but to surpass you."

I'm not sure how to respond. She's not saying she wants me. She wants someone better than me. And now she has him because I gave him to her on a fucking silver platter.

I get what she's saying because at the charity ball last year, I knew I'd already found everything I was looking for in a woman with her.

Full stop.

There is no need for me to look for my soul mate. I know who she is. For me, there is no way for anyone to ever surpass Darcy. She's it for me. And if the only thing I can ever be is her best friend, then that's what I'll be.

Of course it all sounded better before today. Before she met a man she might consider to be the one. Now that she has met him, I'm not sure I can stand by and watch her become someone else's.

"Did my phone drop you?" she asks.

"No," I answer quickly. "I was just thinking about how right you are with that last thing you said because I feel the same way about you."

She lets out another sigh, but this time she sounds all blissed out. "I still can't get over how amazing Tate is. I don't think I can ever repay you for setting us up."

"Are you seeing him again soon?" I squeeze my eyes shut as if doing so will stop me from hearing how wonderful Tate is. She doesn't have to answer my question. Of course she'll be seeing him soon. Tate would be an idiot and a half not to set up another date. While some people would question his sanity after he turned down the contract from New York, one could understand where he was coming from even if they would have reacted differently. However, if he hasn't asked her for another date, I'll personally have him committed.

"Yes." Her voice is excited. "He said he was coming back this way next weekend and wanted to know if we could do dinner. Especially since we had to cancel our reservation for tonight."

"I still can't believe he took you to feed the homeless." Outside of Kara, I can't see any of my recent dates doing anything like that. In fact, I'm guessing a few of them would not only turn their nose up, but also refuse to go.

This is the type of woman you've been dating lately. Shallow and selfish. All at once I feel ashamed. I'm better than this.

"I know," Darcy's saying. "I couldn't believe it either, but it was such a good way to get to know each other. Very unconventional. I like it so much better than the same old, same old, you know?"

"Mmm," I hum. "Somehow I don't know if Alice would have enjoyed it as much as you did."

It hit me that I would never want to do anything like that with Alice. Darcy? Yes, definitely. One of the main reasons would be to watch her as she interacts with people. I envy Tate for that. He was able to see that part of her. She's such a people person and everyone she's ever met loves her.

"Are you talking about O2? That worthless excuse for a woman isn't going to do anything that doesn't directly benefit her." She takes a deep breath. "I know it didn't work out with Kara, and even though I know it could if you'd try one more time, I understand why you won't. And I'm pretty sure you'll never let me set you up again, but Elliott, please, promise me you'll try to find someone worthy of you."

"I promise," I tell her, but only because that's what she wants to hear. Though I admit the thought of dating some like Alice again turns my stomach.

Not wanting to think about dating anyone who isn't Darcy and likewise, not wanting to think about Darcy dating anyone that isn't me, I change the subject. "Are you going to let me take you out for your birthday?"

Her birthday is this upcoming Thursday. I always take her out, assuming we're both in town, which isn't always the case.

She hesitates and I picture her biting her bottom lip. "Mom's actually going to be here on Thursday. And Tate's taking me out on Friday."

"I'm third on the list this year?" I tease to cover up how I really feel. "That's okay, I can handle it. Can you and I do something Saturday?"

"Yes," she says and I hear something in her voice, but can't tell what it is.

"If you're busy," I reply because I honestly can't tell if she's trying to get out of going anywhere with me, "it's okay. We can always go out another time."

"No. Saturday should be fine."

I leave it at that, but I can't help but feel as if she's not telling me something.

CHAPTER ELEVEN: DARCY

"I WASN'T KISSING HER, I WAS
WHISPERING IN HER MOUTH."
CHICO MARX

*T*ate picks me up the next Friday night. He grins as he tells me he doesn't have anything planned for tonight other than dinner. I laugh and follow him out to his car. Like the weekend before, he's a complete gentleman. He opens doors for me. Holds out my chair at the restaurant. On another guy his manners might come across as fake, but like everything else about Tate, they are one hundred percent real.

I'm thankful for the time to sit down and talk with him, just the two of us. It's nice not having to share him with other people. I don't begrudge him the date last weekend, we had fun, did some good, and met some truly wonderful people, but I'm glad I have him to myself tonight.

He's made reservations at a small family owned Italian place. I've never been but I've heard our local hotels recommend it to guests. All it takes is for me to eat a bite of their homemade bread and I know I'm in love.

Tate watches me with laughing eyes. "Good?"

"Beyond good," I say. It wouldn't do for me to eat the entire loaf, although it is small enough I could eat it and still have room for my entree. I make myself remain in my chair and not grab the last piece.

Although, if I eat it, maybe the server will bring more.

"Tell me," Tate says, utterly oblivious to my bread dilemma. "Did you grow up in Atlanta?"

"Yes, right next door to Elliott actually."

"I was wondering how you two met."

I laugh thinking back on that time. "I was in the backyard with my mom, trying to decide where to put my swing set. Elliott comes out of his back door, looks at me, and runs back inside yelling, 'Of course, it's a stinking girl. I told you.'"

"Poor Elliott," Tate says on a chuckle.

"It didn't take him long to get over the fact I was a stinking girl. I could build awesome towers and we'd gang up on his little sister."

"I didn't realize the two of you had that much history. He's told me before that you were his best friend. I suppose I always pictured the two of you as a couple."

I drop my head and pretend to be busy wiping the breadcrumbs off the table. "No, we've never dated each other."

I expect him to ask me why that is. It's the next logical question, after all. But he doesn't. "Elliott said you traveled a lot for your job and quite a bit of it was international. Have you ever been to Italy?"

"Only once and so far it's my favorite out of all the countries I've visited." I'd love to go back someday. It's a beautiful country and I remember when I was there thinking how much Elliott would love it.

"I've never been there," Tate says and in my mind I leave Italy and Elliott to return to Tate and Atlanta. Somehow it's not the same.

. . .

THE FOLLOWING MORNING, I can't help but think that something's not right. It's annoying because I can't decide what it is.

It's not that dinner the night before wasn't great. It was and I'm starting to get the impression it'll always be that way with Tate. He's an amazing guy and I find I'm more and more attracted to him each time we talk or go out. And yet there's this nagging suspicion I can't shake that I'm somehow not right for him. Part of it goes back to what I told him on our first date—I'm not good enough. But he's never made me feel that way.

To be honest, I don't know what my problem is. Maybe I'll ask Elliott about it tonight. Just the thought of him makes me smile.

My phone rings, and my stomach drops when I see it's my supervisor's personal number.

"Meredith," I say, hoping against hope the call doesn't mean what I think it does.

"Darcy," she says. "I hate to bother you on a Saturday, but the Hoffman Group is in town and their Account Executive has had a family emergency. I need you to be with them for the tour this afternoon and dinner tonight."

"I'd love to Meredith, but I have plans tonight."

"I understand," she says, but then she takes a deep breath. "I've never asked you to do this, but I need you to rearrange your plans. This is very important. I wouldn't ask you to otherwise."

"If it's so important, wouldn't it be better for you to fill in?"

"I'm in California."

I close my eyes. I'm going to have to cancel on Elliott.

Damn it all. The one person I can be myself with and not have to worry about what he thinks or how I'm being perceived.

Reluctantly, I tell Meredith I'll do it. She's all happy and full of sunshine and happiness. I have to tell her goodbye before I say something I'll regret. I disconnect and wait for her to send over my new itinerary for the night. Once I have it, I call Elliott. As expected, he's less than pleased, though he tries to cover it.

"It's okay, Darc," he says. "I get it. I've had to cancel on you before because of work, too." He's saying the right words, but I can hear the disappointment in his voice.

"Once," I remind him. "Two years ago. And roads were closed due to a hurricane and major flooding."

He chuckles, but it's not a happy sound. "I'm trying to make you feel better, but if you want me to be an ass and remind you that technically I'm your third date of the week so it really doesn't matter if you blow me off, I can."

Ouch. "We can do tomorrow night."

"Actually, we can't," he says. "I have a prep meeting to go over the agenda for the prospects meetings next week."

"That's your problem, not mine," I tell him. "I'm telling you I'm free."

"I'm available next Wednesday," he says. "Does that work for you?"

I'm not happy about next Wednesday. I'm not happy I have to wait that long to have dinner with my best friend. Being around him has always made me feel calmer and grounded me for lack of better words. "Next Wednesday will be perfect."

"No," he says softly and the warmth of his tone calms me. "Wednesday will not be perfect, but I'm pretty sure we can come close."

I have no idea what he means by that, but I'm not going to give him any indication that I don't know.

"Now," he says, his voice just as low. "What time do you have to run off to play tour and dinner guide?"

I glance at the clock in my home office. The only wall clock in my house. I'd refused to leave it behind when I moved here from my old apartment. In today's tech crazy world where you're only as good as your most recent gadget, I miss the steady hands of a watch or the rhythmic tick tock of a wall clock. But no time to dwell on clocks at the moment. Elliott had asked a question.

"Around two hours," I tell him, and it hits me again just how much I do not want to do this tonight. I want to be Elliott's date because I realize how very rarely we've seen each other lately. I almost ask if he'd like to come by my place after I finish work, but I stop myself before saying the words, mainly because I don't know what time I'll be finished. He has a key to my townhouse, so if I ended up being later than I thought, he could wait for me inside. But still, it's not fair for me to ask him to do that.

"I'd better let you go," he says, bringing me back to the here and now. "I know all too well how early you want to be."

I laugh because it's true and say goodbye, wishing it was already Wednesday and I'd be seeing Elliott soon and not a bunch of people I didn't know. I hate the disappointment he wasn't able to disguise in his voice and the fact that it's only there because of me.

Unfortunately, it's only Saturday. I take a deep breath that sounds more like a sigh than anything else and force myself to start getting ready.

. . .

ELLIOTT SENDS me a text halfway through dinner. As soon as my phone buzzes in my pocket, I excuse myself and go to the restroom. I smile when I pull it out and see his name.

I know you're doing Boring Business Shit, but how about I drop by your place around 11? It'll be like college. Our old favorite show is live tonight. It's new.

I think college might have been the last time we watched Saturday night comedy together. *Damn, when did I get so old?*

I respond quickly.

OMG. YES!

He answers with a smiley face and I walk out of the restroom in a much better mood knowing I'll be able to see Elliott after this dinner is over.

IT's after eleven by the time I make it home, and it's crazy how happy I am to see Elliott waiting for me on my couch when I walk in. Everything is all set out: beer for him, wine for me, and he's even pulled out my favorite fuzzy socks.

I drop my purse and briefcase on the floor as soon as I lock the door behind me. I make my way over to Elliott who stands as I walk toward him. "You are amazing," I say, throwing my arms around his neck and giving him a peck on the cheek. "Why some woman hasn't snatched you up already, I'll never know."

He chuckles and pulls away quicker than he normally does. "Crazy woman," he says. "Why do I need someone else when I have you?"

"Sex?" I answer. "I'm going to go change real quick."

It's not until I'm in my bedroom that I realize he never

responded to my sex answer. That's not really like him. If there's one subject he can go on and on about, it's sex. I tilt my head. Now that I think about it, outside of the oral sex chat we had before the dates, it's been ages since he's talked about sex.

Probably because he's getting so much of it from his plastic girls.

But I don't think he's seeing anyone. At least not anyone that he's mentioned to me. And again that's not typical.

I'm not going to think about it anymore. Tonight we're simply going to be two old friends spending some chill time over television and drinks. Whatever's going on between Elliott and the women he dates is none of my business.

HALFWAY THROUGH THE SHOW, Elliott mutes the TV. Neither one of us is crazy about the band that's going to play. I'm sprawled out on the couch with my feet in his lap because he confiscated my fuzzy socks while I was changing and I decided to be a brat and plopped my feet there. He eventually pulled the socks out and put them on my feet, but I never moved them.

"So tell me why a hot catch like you is sitting on my couch on a Saturday night?" I wiggle my toes at him.

"The hot date I had lined up supposedly had to go into work." He grabs one of my wiggly toes to still it and begins to rub my foot.

"Supposedly? You don't believe her?" I'm trying to concentrate on the conversation, but damn his hands feel good.

"I believe her. After all, the guy she's dating lives out of town and she saw him last night. I didn't have a chance to find someone else on such short notice."

My brain works itself out of the haze of pleasure his hands have expertly sent me into. "Dating? Is that what Tate and I are doing?"

"Aren't you?" He cocks an eyebrow at me. "You aren't dating anyone else and I don't think he is either."

"That's not because we've agreed to be exclusive or anything," I tell him. I'm just a bit frazzled at the thought of being that serious with Tate after two dates. "I mean, he hasn't even really kissed me." That last part slips out. My plan had been to keep that detail to myself.

"What?" Elliott's eyes grow wide. "He hasn't kissed you yet?"

I pull my feet from his lap, embarrassed but I'm not sure why. "He said he wanted to take things slow."

"There's taking thing slow and then there's letting a good thing slip away because you're a fucking idiot."

"I thought it was sort of sweet." Or at least that's what I tried to convince myself anyway.

Elliott looks at me the way I envision he'd look at somebody who asked how many innings were in a basketball game or how many touchdowns a baseball player made. "Darcy," he says, using that *let me explain how everything that just came out of your mouth is batshit crazy* voice. "Sweet is bringing you flowers or picking up all the ingredients for and baking a cake to surprise you when you've had a bad day. Not kissing you after the second date is downright certifiable."

He sounds angry, and all I can picture now is him on the phone with Tate asking why the hell he hasn't kissed me. And then Tate would know I'd told Elliott about it. Complained even.

"Promise me you won't call and bug Tate about it," I plead with him.

"Hell, no, I'm not bringing it up to him." He's definitely angry. "If he wants to fuck up the best thing he's ever been given, it's all on him. I'm not going to help him fix it. He can figure it out his own damn self." He mumbles something under his breath, but the only words I can pick up are 'kiss' and 'idiot.'

"So tell me, you badass dating expert," I say. "Do you kiss on the first date?"

He raises an eyebrow and I'm pretty sure he's going to tell me it doesn't matter what he does, but instead he crooks a finger at me. "Come here."

Both of us are already sitting on the couch, so we're fairly close to begin with, but to make him happy and keep him talking, I scoot toward him to where we're almost touching. We both turn so we're facing each other.

"Usually, yes," he says. He moves his arm closest to the couch to where it rests along the top and his fingers brush my shoulder. "But there are no hard and fast rules when it comes to the first kiss. It all depends on her."

As he talks, he slowly inches his fingers, barely touching me, but I'm hyperaware of where he is and what his fingers are doing. Need and arousal flood my body at the same time. I'm confused as shit because this is Elliott and my body's not supposed to be reacting this way to him.

But my body doesn't seem to care; it wants Elliott. He lightly strokes my cheek and works his fingers into my hair. "I look for signs, hints that she wants a kiss. Sometimes she'll part her lips. Other times it's more subtle. Maybe she's looking at my lips."

I actually am staring at his mouth, so when he says that, I look up and catch his eyes. He smiles, but it's nothing like any smile I've ever seen on him before. This smile is seductive. It's an entirely different Elliott I've never known, but I want to.

Does he feel it, this pulsing energy between us? Then I think, how could he not, with the heat of it almost burning me while we sit here on my couch? "Elliott," I start and stop because I have no idea what to say.

Not that it would matter if I did. He places his free finger across my lips. "Shhh."

For some reason, his touch and command to be silent are the most erotic things I've ever experienced and a low moan escapes from my throat.

"Fuck," Elliott replies just as low, and he clenches my hair tighter.

His finger is still lightly resting on my lips and we both seem to realize it at the same time. I don't move because for a second, it's as if he's looking directly into my soul, and he sees himself reflected there. He shifts his fingers so his thumb traces my lips. His touch is both exactly as I imagined, while somehow being completely different.

"Darcy," he says and that's all it takes. I lean forward at the same time he does.

We shouldn't be here like this. Shouldn't be sitting this close to each other on the couch we've both sat on probably a million times. Because nothing about those times is any way similar to what we're doing right now.

His lips are inches from mine and I suddenly want them more than I've ever wanted anything. I've imagined them so many times: how they feel and what they taste like. Would his kiss be soft or hard? Would he be gentle or demanding?

It doesn't matter. I just want him. Elliott.

He brushes his mouth across mine so gently, I actually open my eyes a bit to make sure I didn't dream the entire thing. I didn't, but he's pulled his head back and my cheeks are hot because I'm pretty sure he hadn't been planning to kiss me.

I open my mouth to apologize, but he surprises me by saying, "I want to do that again."

"Yes," I whisper so softly I'm not sure he hears.

This time he frames my face with his hands. A twinge of guilt grabs me by the throat, but I close my eyes and will it to go away. Then his mouth is on mine again, but this time his lips are harder and more demanding and *holy mother of pearl*, how in the world is it possible for me to not know Elliott is a master kisser?

He takes his time, placing soft kisses against my mouth, while in the same breath, nibbling my lips with just enough pressure from his teeth to have me nearly writhing. I want him. I want him to nibble every inch of my body. I want to spread my legs and have him eat me out the way he described it before.

I whimper, imagining it. He pulls back long enough to whisper, "I know what you're thinking about." His voice is coarse and rough, and it feels good to know he's as affected as I am. He bites down on my earlobe and gives it a tug that sends a jolt of electricity straight to my clit.

I gasp in unexpected pleasure. No one has ever done that to me before, and Elliott tilts my head back with the hand he has in my hair. I close my eyes and simply feel: his lips covering mine, demanding entrance, his body shifting, pressing to get closer when I part my lips and let him in.

He doesn't hesitate, accepting my invitation to deepen the kiss. His tongue sweeps inside my mouth. It's so easy to picture another part of him inside me, and I place a hand on his upper thigh and slowly drag it up to rest on his erection.

He feels so much bigger than I'd imagined. I can't help

but whisper, "Oh my, God," as I move my fingers along the hard, denim-clad ridge. Unfortunately, my amazement at the size of his dick makes him pull back. His eyes widen.

"Damn, Darcy," he says and scoots much too far away. "I'm sorry."

I want to tell him it's okay. That I liked it. That I didn't want him to stop. And most of all, that there is nothing in the world to apologize for. But one glance at his face stops me in my tracks. He's running his fingers through his hair, trying to straighten it up, and looking over everything in the room except me.

"Elliott," I finally whisper.

He turns his attention to me and his eyes are careful and intent while he studies me. I'm not sure exactly what he's searching for. If it's guilt, he won't find any. He won't find remorse or regret either. Though it saddens me that all three are apparent in his expression. Is it because he thinks I'm Tate's or is it something else altogether?

"I'm sorry," he repeats, and this time adding, "I don't know what got into me, but it won't happen again."

Frankly, that only makes me mad. "Would you stop apologizing?" I ask him. "You act as if that kiss was all you, but from where I sat, there were two of us, and we seemed to be enjoying ourselves. Or at least I was."

"Just because we were enjoying ourselves doesn't mean it was right or that we should keep doing it." He obviously sees my anger because he takes a deep breath and when he speaks again, he sounds very calm. "Darcy, you're my best friend in entire world. You have been since we were what, six or seven? You are everything to me. I can replace a lover in my bed, but I can't replace you."

I can't be angry at him for speaking those thoughts, not when they are the exact same ones I had not long ago. Had I not come to the same conclusion? That I can't replace Elliott?

He's right, and even though my body is still protesting, calling a stop to what we were doing before we went any further was the right thing to do. My body can and will get over not sleeping with him tonight. My heart would never get over losing him. A whole night of pleasure in his arms isn't worth not being best friends after.

For several minutes we both sit on the couch. If I was sitting with anyone else in this position, the silence would be awkward. After how Elliott and I spent the last fifteen minutes the silence between the two of us should be awkward. For some reason, however, it's not.

It all goes back to how well Elliott and I know each other and how comfortable we are with each other. But all I have to do is glance to my side, though, and see that Elliott's erection isn't completely gone. That one glance and it's perfectly clear I don't know everything about him.

He catches me taking a peek at his crotch and grins. I laugh. For this one minute, everything is okay. We're okay. Because even though we were tempted, we didn't succumb, and if there are emotional ramifications, we'll deal with them. I take a deep breath, and it hits me how close I came to losing him by being stupid.

There's an obnoxious voice in the back of my head whispering that even if we haven't called ourselves exclusive and even if he hasn't really kissed me, I would still feel like I'd cheated on Tate. And though it's much much too early to even think such things, Tate is the type of man I always pictured myself settling down with.

Elliott stands up. The television show is long over, and it's time for us both to go to bed. Alone. He walks over and takes my hand and I go with him to the door. He doesn't open it and leave how I expected, though. He further surprises me by taking me in his arms and gently holding me. It's a stark contrast to how we were on the couch and yet, still comforting.

But even that surprise is nothing compared to my shock when he whispers, "Even though it shouldn't have happened, I'm glad it did. That was the best kiss I've ever had."

I'm speechless as he lightly strokes my cheek and walks away. I lock the door behind him and when I crawl into bed moments later, it's never felt so lonely.

CHAPTER TWELVE: ELLIOTT

"THE FIRST DUTY OF LOVE IS TO LISTEN."
PAUL TILLICH

I keep telling myself that the kiss hasn't changed anything and Darcy and I are the same as ever, but for every time I tell myself that, there are two more where I recall every tiny detail about the kiss. It doesn't take much for me to remember. Oftentimes I find the memory is triggered by the simplest of things: a passing fragrance, the sound of laughter, the breath of anything soft against me. That's all it takes, and I'm back on Darcy's couch with her in my arms. She is soft and needy against me. She's desperate and she wants me, as much as I want her.

I want her more than I want anything.

At night, when I'm alone in bed, because I'm always sleeping alone these days, if I close my eyes, I can still feel her around me. I feel her fingers tickling my inner thighs; I know where she is taking them. And I want her there. Her fingers. Her mouth. Anything.

That night on her couch, I forced myself to back away, knowing that if I didn't, I would take her every single way I had ever dreamed of taking her. So I made myself stop. Even in bed by myself, I won't go down those fantasy paths anymore. Too much heartache, wanting things that will never happen.

Unfortunately, as much as Darcy and I had said we would stop so that things wouldn't be awkward between us, things are different. I'm not able to name what it is exactly that's changed, but it's there, all the same. It's very strange. We still talk on the phone, we still text, but there's a difference in it, an *awareness* perhaps. I don't know. All I know is I miss my best friend and want her back badly.

It's been two weeks, and we haven't seen each other face-to-face since that night. It kills me, because before too long, she'll be headed out of town. Usually I know her schedule like the back my hand, but she hasn't sent one to me lately. I'm afraid to call and find out why. I'm afraid I've lost her. It hurts to think about her, but I can't stop.

If Darcy in my fantasies months ago kept me awake, thinking she might not be my best friend anymore won't let me get to sleep at all. Of course, I haven't asked her to see me face-to-face. It didn't used to be this hard. Seriously, we've been friends for how many years? It's never taken any thought or effort. If I want to see her I would go and see her. But now it seems everything has an underlying meaning. Or at least every time I think about going by to see her or asking her to meet me for dinner, I catch myself wondering if she'll see or take something the wrong way.

Add to that, the fact that she is still seeing Tate, and I'm a complete basket case.

I don't know how many dates they've been on; I'm quite positive he's kissed her by now. The thought of someone else kissing her makes me want to punch something. Instead, I've been working out my frustrations in the gym. The team is better because of it, and I'm in the best shape I've been in since... well, a long time.

It's Saturday night and I'm alone in my apartment eating a frozen dinner I cooked in the microwave. The meal is horrible; it tastes like plastic and I can barely chew it for fear of chipping a tooth. I stand up from the stool at my kitchen island and throw it away, disgusted at both the dinner and myself. I need to do something before I turn into a recluse who only communicates with grunts.

Tomorrow is Sunday. Sunday is the only day Darcy allows herself to sleep in late. Unless she has plans, she rarely gets out of bed before ten. I'm going to be at her house tomorrow at ten-thirty and take her to brunch. It will be a light and breezy day, no talk of kisses or what might've been. We'll be completely normal and by the end of the day, it'll be like that kiss never happened.

As PLANNED, the next day I arrive at her townhouse promptly at ten-thirty. I'm feeling great. The sun is shining, there's no rain called for anytime soon, heck, even the humidity isn't bad. I park my car and hop up the stairs to her front door. I feel so good I'm actually humming. I ring the doorbell and then knock on the door for good measure. "Wake up, lazy tail, I'm taking you out for brunch."

I'm smiling as the door opens, but it's not my best friend and the most beautiful person in the entire world who answers the door. Oh no, the universe isn't that nice to me. It's Tate.

Fucking. Tate.

Opening her door.

We stare at each other in stunned silence.

I should probably say something, but I don't know what. Take, likewise, looks equally confused.

"Tate," Darcy yells from the bedroom. "Who was at the door?"

She walks toward us and Tate opens the door further to let me in.

"It's Elliott," he says.

I step inside, ignoring Tate. I have to or else I'll punch him because I'm pretty sure the fucker has kissed her by now. They've probably gone further, but I don't allow myself to think about that just yet. I focus on Darcy.

She's gorgeous, of course, and dressed to go out. She's wearing my favorite sundress, the blue one that makes her look divine and she's curled her hair, which she rarely does, but always makes her look even more stunning. I can compliment her dress or her hair. I can tell her I was just in the neighborhood and decided to stop by. But it's clear what I need to do, and I sure as hell don't want to do it, but so help me, God, I will.

I take a deep breath and make sure I'm not looking at either of them when I speak. "I obviously came at a bad time. Thought I'd surprise you, but joke's on me because you surprised me instead. That's what I get for not calling first. It won't happen again." I pause and then start to laugh. I can't help it. "Sorry, I seem to be saying that a lot. *It won't happen again.*"

I risk a glance at Darcy and she looks absolutely mortified. Her mouth is hanging open and her face is all red. Even worse, she's so close to tears, I have to turn away. I don't look at Tate. "I'm so sorry Darc," I whisper. "For everything."

I stride out the door and down her driveway as quickly as possible without it being considered a run. I'm a fucking moron. What the hell is the matter with me?

"Elliott," someone calls from the house, but it's not her. It's *him*.

I think about continuing, but I stop because I have to man up. I am, after all, the one responsible for this. I'm the one who pushed them together. I didn't know it was going to be so painful.

Tate is from Tallulah Falls. He obviously spent the night.

"Elliott." He's by my side and reaches out to touch my arm. "I thought I asked. I'm sorry, I didn't know."

"Didn't know what?" I don't know what the fuck he's talking about.

He takes a deep breath and I watch him, curious as to what he's going to say. "I didn't know you were in love with her."

CHAPTER THIRTEEN: DARCY

"GIVE ME ONE FRIEND, JUST ONE, WHO
MEETS THE NEEDS OF ALL MY VARYING
MOODS." ESTHER M. CLAR

I watch Tate run after Elliott from my front windows while at the same time I'm fighting to keep my tears at bay. Tate catches up to him and Elliott actually stops to talk. I hold my breath, ready to run outside if Elliott hits him. I'm pretty sure he will, he had that look. That is when he wasn't looking at me as if I'd ripped his heart out of his chest and stomped on it while he watched. I've never seen that look before and I hope to never see it again.

As soon as he stormed out, I'd all but yelled at Tate to go get him and bring him back. I have to hand it to Tate, he didn't hesitate a second before running after him. I stand in awe as the two of them continue to talk. What in the world are they discussing?

The obvious answer is, of course, me or at least some combination of subjects pertaining to me. However, in the time I've been seeing Tate, I've come to learn that he is very private. I doubt he will tell Elliott much, if anything, about our relationship.

The fact Elliott hasn't punched him yet leads me to

believe Tate at least told him we haven't slept together, regardless of the fact that Tate had spent the night under my roof last night. To be honest, I'm still working that one out for myself because had Tate given me any hint he was down for it, I'd have been all over him last night.

Part of me feels as if I should thank Tate for claiming my guest room so quickly and setting boundaries that didn't include sex. I haven't made up my mind yet if I really want to sleep with Tate or if I just want to try and erase the kiss with Elliott. Realistically, nothing will erase it and even thinking that is enough of a reason for me to stay out Tate's bed.

But, I can't lie, another part of me feels like the world's biggest skank for thinking about sleeping with Tate when he's nowhere near that same page. I long to sit down and talk this feeling I have out with Elliott. In the past, it would never cross my mind not to discuss it with him. All of that was before The Kiss, of course. The kiss that was never supposed to happen and yet it did and in doing so, it rocked my world so hard, I've yet to recover.

In my driveway, Tate and Elliott are making their way back toward my house with Tate leading the way. I step out of the window so it won't appear as if I've been spying and smooth nonexistent wrinkles from my dress. At least I don't feel like crying at the moment.

Tate makes it inside first and is all smiles, while Elliott looks like a condemned man on his way to the executioner. "I asked Elliott to join us for brunch." Tate sounds cheerfully optimistic announcing this, but I catch a hint of worry in his voice, he probably doesn't want anyone to notice it, but oh, well.

"Thank you, Tate," I say and finally look at Elliott. His expression is void of emotion. He's good and he can do that with his facial features, but he can't do anything about his eyes. His eyes tell the truth about what this brunch will cost him and I'm humbled.

"It's nothing, Darcy," Tate says. "Why don't you ride with Elliott, and I'll drive separate so I can call ahead and revise our reservation to three?"

I look to Elliott to try to discern if he knew Tate would do this, but he gives nothing away, so I say, "Sure," much brighter than I feel.

Elliott remains silent until we're both in his car and on the highway. "You know Tate is already half in love with you?"

I snort. "I doubt that."

"I'm a man. I know these things."

"Did you know he spent the night in my house last night and nothing, and by nothing, I mean not one thing happened?"

His grip on the steering wheel tightens and his knuckles turn white. "He may have mentioned it."

I can't think of a reply to follow that, so I take another direction. "I'm really glad you're joining us."

Now it's his turn to snort. "Said no one ever to their third wheel best friend who crashed their brunch date."

I cross my arms. I hate it when he's in a pissy mood. "You know, if you're going to be a jerk, you can just drop me off at the door and drive yourself home. I don't enjoy being around you when you're like this."

"Then there will be two of us who don't want to be there."

I also hate it when we argue while he's driving because I can't see his expression. "Then why did you agree to come in the first place?"

"I guess I can't turn Tate down either. Oh, wait, you didn't get the chance to turn him down, did you?

Damn it all, did Tate tell him every last detail about our relationship? He moves his head and I can see just enough of his face to tell he's smirking. "Why are you being such an ass?"

He sobers up at that. "I am, aren't I? I'm sorry."

I give a half grunt. "No, you aren't."

"I am because it distresses you and I never want to be the cause of that." He presses his lips together before adding, "It's just...I miss you, is all. And I had today all planned out for just the two of us and I show up to get you and *he's* there."

"Two things," I say, but I should really say three, because that might be part of his problem, but I don't believe for a minute that's the whole of it. "One, you never called me about today, you simply showed up. And two, what's wrong with Tate? You've been out with me and dates before, not to mention you're the one who set us up."

He waits a few seconds before answering. "I think with those other guys, it never felt real. And Tate, I don't know, he seems different. I can actually see you with him. I keep thinking, no matter what I do, one way or another, I'm going to end up losing you."

I feel sad all at once, because I can sense it as well. Things are changing. I don't know if it all has to do with Tate, but something elemental is different about Elliott and I. Would it still be that way if we hadn't kissed? I don't know. I know one thing, though. I put my hand on his knee. "No matter what happens and no matter who I end up with, you will never lose me."

That actually gets a smile out of him. "Thanks, Darc."

The tension leaves my body and I'm actually able to

return his smile. "However, all bets are off if you marry O2. If that happens, you'll never see me again."

He glances at me with such a look of horror that I laugh and once I start, I'm unable to stop. Elliott finds this hysterical and pretty soon, he's laughing as well. And that's what we're doing when we pull up to the valet stand at the restaurant.

Tate arches an eyebrow, but otherwise seems relieved. About what? I'm not sure and it won't do any good to ask either man, because neither of them will tell me.

CHAPTER FOURTEEN: ELLIOTT

"THE COMPATIBILITY OF A COUPLE AND
THE QUALITY OF A RELATIONSHIP LIES IN
THE WAY THEY HANDLE THEIR
ARGUMENTS AND DIFFERENCES." NISHAN
PANWAR

"*I didn't know you were in love with her.*"

Tate's words echo in my head during brunch. I've been under the assumption that I've managed to hide my feelings where Darcy is concerned. However, if Tate can see through my façade and so quickly realize the truth, I'm sure Darcy will as well. If she looks hard enough, that is.

Maybe she won't. I'm pretty certain Tate isn't going to tell her. Not only did I manage to lie my ass off and finally convince him I'm not in love with her, he confided that he believes she might be The One. I smiled and told him I was happy for him and that's when he invited me to brunch.

Because I'm a glutton for punishment, I accepted. Now I get to spend the next hour or so watching Darcy and the man I'm sure is going to take my place in her life and heart. As soon as we walk into the restaurant, everyone is staring at them. Of course they are. They are beautiful together. Anyone who looks long enough will also see how well they interact. The little smiles she gives him, the way he trips all over himself to get whatever she needs. It's so sickening sweet.

It's enough to drive me to drinking.

I don't drink anything other than tea, though, because I don't want to ruin this for her. Darcy is my heart and soul and this is such a simple thing to give her. I might as well get used to it. If she ends up with Tate, I'll have to do this a lot in the future. Might as well practice now.

I'm only half listening to their conversation, especially when the server comes over to refill my tea. Then Darcy says something that grabs my attention.

"What was that?" I ask.

"Which part?" She arches a perfect eyebrow at me when I don't answer. "You haven't been listening at all, have you?"

I point to my tea. "I was thirsty; I've been trying to flag someone down."

She doesn't believe me, but tells me anyway. "Tate and I were talking about next weekend. I'm going to take a few days off and go visit him in the mountains."

It hits me then that this relationship is more serious than I thought. "You are? But you've been home for over a month. Isn't it time for you to jet off somewhere for work?"

She shakes her head. "I'm at home at least until the first of the year. And I've also requested a change in assignment so I can stay in Atlanta for most of the time. All that travel gets old, you know?"

Yes, in fact, I do know. What I don't know is how it is that I don't know any of this. We've always exchanged schedules. We've always had to because both of us travel so much. Expect now it appears as if I'll be the only one.

But it's more than that. Based on what she just said, she's changing jobs and didn't tell me. I didn't even know she was thinking about it. That realization cuts deep as it sinks in she's not telling me things she would have in the past. I work hard not to let this show. "I didn't know you disliked it enough to change jobs. When did that happen?"

"Just a few days ago, really." She shrugs like it's no big deal and I nod as if to say I totally get it, but on the inside I'm screaming.

Today, she doesn't tell me she's changing jobs. What will she not tell me a week from now? A month? I suddenly lose my appetite.

When I'm eighty I'll still be beating myself up for setting her up with Tate.

Except, I won't. As long as he treats her well and makes her happy, I'll be happy for her. I know her well enough to know she'll never cut me out of her life. One day if she and Tate have kids, I can be their cool Uncle Elliott. I lie and tell myself that'll be enough, but I'm not buying it. If being Uncle Elliott won't be enough, what do I want? To be her kid's dad?

The room tilts as I think about that. I've never even thought about having kids, yet here I am eating brunch with Darcy and her boyfriend and suddenly I'm thinking about her and I having kids? What the hell?

But once the thought is in my head, it won't leave. It's almost as if I can see them. There are three. The oldest is a girl and then there are twin boys.

Across the table, Tate is laughing at something Darcy says. They both look at me and Darcy wrinkles her forehead. "Are you okay Elliott?" she asks. "You look like you've seen a ghost."

"I'm fine," I lie. "Just felt a little lightheaded there for a minute. I'm better already."

She doesn't look convinced. "Are you sure? Do we need to leave? Should I call you a cab?"

I shake my head.

"He's a grown man," Tate says. "If he says he's fine, he's fine."

Conversation stalls after that. We finish eating, not saying much until the bill comes and Tate and I fight over who's going to pick it up. Tate is momentarily distracted and it's enough for me to grab the check.

"Hey, Darcy," Tate says. "Isn't that the woman I met at your office last week?"

"Shit," Darcy says under her breath, and I look up to see Kara heading our way with a guy behind her.

"Hey, Kara," Tate says as they come to our table. "Good to see you. I'd offer to let you sit with us, but we've just finished."

"That's okay," Kara says. "Hi, Darcy. Elliott."

I can't help but notice her expression cools a bit as she looks at me. I'm not sure why. I mean, it's not like I poured *my* beer all over her and I wasn't the one who was ridiculously late.

"Nice to see you, Kara," I say with as big a smile as I can get away with.

"This is Dan," Kara says, introducing the man at her side. He's slightly taller than me, but he has an air about him that seems fake. I peg him either as a news anchor or an actor. "He works for News Eleven," she finishes.

He shakes Tate and Darcy's hands and seems nice enough. Until he turns to me with the world's dorkiest grin. "So you're Elliott? I've heard a lot about you."

CHAPTER FIFTEEN: DARCY

"YOU DON'T FIND LOVE, IT FINDS YOU."
ANAÏS NIN

The Friday afternoon after brunch I'm driving up to Tate's camp. It's about a three-hour drive and the time alone in the car allows me to think. I see this weekend as a kind of like 'Do or Die' for Tate and me. He's a good guy and all, but I don't feel passionate about him. I suppose that's not necessary, I mean, a lot of people don't have passionate relationships all the time. That's okay, right?

I don't know. Lately, it seems I don't know anything at all. Everything is so confusing. Even the things that used to be simple, like Elliott. Why do I feel more passion toward Elliott than I do Tate? It doesn't make any sense. I can't help but think maybe it's because I've known him for so long.

Then I think about that kiss.

Granted, I'm not a prude, and I don't come close to the other end of the spectrum, but I've dated my share of guys, and I've kissed most of them. No one, not one single one, as ever come close to affecting me the way Elliott's kiss did. I shouldn't think about the kiss, because once I do, I won't be able to stop. Thinking about Elliott and his kiss while I'm with Tate is not a good idea.

I force myself to stop thinking about Elliott and focus my attention on Tate and the upcoming weekend. Tate has kissed me. It's nothing earth shattering. Hell, it's not even earth tilting. But it was nice. I sigh. Is that what I want? *Nice?* I don't know.

I don't have a parental relationship to look up to. I know some people whose parents have been married forty or fifty years. But not mine, and not Elliott's either. If I had that, an example to look up to, maybe I'd know what a marriage should look like. I don't. All I have are books and TV.

Maybe that's what my problem is. Maybe, I've watched too many movies, read too many books, and have a misguided and delusional thoughts on what marriage should look like. Maybe nice is okay. If that's the case, I should be completely and head over heels happy with Tate.

But I can't help think that there's something more. That marriage is something more. That love is something more. And nice is nothing but settling. And I don't want to settle. I want it all. I want the fairytale, happy ending, happily ever after, and the to be continued. I want fireworks and explosions. I want fights and making up. And I want sex, lots and lots of dirty, nasty, loving, passionate sex.

So the question for this weekend is, am I getting that with Tate? And if not, can I live with nice?

It's those two questions that have driven me insane all week, that kept me from sleep, and that I spent way too much time obsessing over. I'm here until Monday. Hopefully by the time I'm driving home on Monday afternoon, I'll know one way or the other if Tate is the one for me. Or if I should just keep looking for something else somewhere down the line.

I can do this. I need to do this. I *will* do this.

SURPRISINGLY, the miles go by quickly as I think about the upcoming weekend and Elliott and Tate. It isn't long before I pull through the camp's gates. The beauty of the area stuns me. All lush and green with wildflowers and tall trees. So different from Atlanta. So peaceful.

Following the directions Tate gave me, I continue along the winding gravel drive and pull into a small parking lot. I stop my car, pleased to see Tate walking toward me.

"Hey," he says. "You made good time."

"Traffic wasn't all that bad," I tell him.

He hugs me and kisses my cheek. I wonder briefly why he does that? Why my cheek and not my lips? The next time I'll move my face and make him kiss my lips.

He pulls away. "Let me get your bags."

I pop open the trunk and gather my purse and laptop while Tate grabs the bigger bags. "This way," he says, leading me to what he calls the guesthouse. He goes on to explain that the small house is more often than not, empty.

I imagine that most people who come with a group, would more than likely stay in the cabins or the dormitories as Tate calls them. He had told me once before he lives in the main building on the campus. Apparently, he has renovated the upper floors into his personal living space. I thought that I would be staying there. I was obviously mistaken.

When I think about it, it makes sense because he would want to set an example. However, it still annoys me a little.

We walk inside the guest house and though it is small, like he'd said, it is clean and cozy. Containing only a small living room, a kitchenette, and a bedroom with an attached bathroom, it has everything I need for the weekend.

"This is lovely," I say, walking toward the back window which is huge and takes up most of the back wall. "I think if I lived here, I'd never want to leave."

He chuckles. "I don't think I could live in the city," he says. "Although, it is good to get away from nature every so often."

"The good thing about getting away, is that when you get home, this is what you have to look forward to."

"Very true," he says and there's pride in his eyes, as he looks over the land that he has claimed as his own.

I learned from talking with him as well as my online research, that he and his staff operate the camp with the children coming in every two to four weeks. On occasion, a few will stay longer than that and a few will stay shorter. They do a lot online to ensure the kids aren't behind in school when they return. There's also a separate meeting area set up in case the children have family come for visits.

I tell Tate to just leave my bags in the bedroom and I'll unpack later, because he wants to show me around the place. He locks the door behind us, and hands me a key that I slip in my pocket.

We take our time as we walk, and I can't help but watch his face light up as he gives me the grand tour. The camp is very quiet and it appears as if we're the only ones out and about. Which is fine by me, at least until I get my bearings.

He owns a few hundred acres. A lot of it is cleared, but there is a fair amount of wooded land as well. He points out four separate dormitories, two for boys and two for girls, each divided by age as well as the staff housing behind them. The main house where he lives, is nearby and also contains a kitchen, dining area, and a meeting room, all on the first floor. There is another separate building for the school and multipurpose rooms. Behind the main house is a smaller building he tells me he hopes to turn into a library/music room soon, if he can get the funding.

The outside activity area is huge as one would expect, complete with a lake for water sports, and a large campfire area he says is a big camp favorite. His voice grows wistful as he shows me the area where he has planned to build a barn to house a few horses. He also mentions he'd like to get a few chickens, but admits it'll be later before he gets serious about doing anything about that. The barn and library/music room, he says, are his next project.

I know from reading online a lot of what he has going on. But I have to admit that I'm shocked and surprised at how much he's taken on. Likewise, I'm impressed at how much he has already accomplished. There are those who thought he made a huge mistake by turning down all the money from New York. However seeing all this, I know he made the right decision. He looks at home here. Much more so than he did in the city.

"Where is everyone?" I ask as he walks me back to the guest house to unpack.

He glances at his watch. "They're just finishing up group sessions and then it'll be free time for about an hour, then dinner. Are you hungry?"

I've been a little bit nervous about meeting the children, as well as the staff that works here. Part of that is because I can't help but wonder how many other women he has brought by this place in the past.

I want to ask Tate if they know I'm here, or if they know about me, period. Unfortunately, I can't think a way to ask without sounding horribly self-important.

"Sure." I smile up at him. "Looking forward to it."

He chuckles, and I don't think he believes me at all.

As it turns out, there's nothing for me to worry about. His staff is friendly and welcoming, and the children are just as nice. In fact, it's a wonderful dinner and I have a great time meeting and talking with everyone. I joke with Tate there is no way I'm going to remember everyone's name. We sit at a table in the middle of everyone, which is good for talking with people, but not necessarily good for private conversation with Tate.

The children are excited because after dinner there's a movie planned outside on a big screen the staff are bringing in. Tate asks if I would like to join, and I tell him of course I do, I haven't driven all this way and taken time off of work to sit in the guest house the entire time by myself.

After we finish eating, the kids run off to their rooms to get ready to watch the movie. Everyone is working or doing something and I feel kind of out of place not doing anything. I tell Tate, and he says we can go help pop popcorn if I would like.

In a way it reminds me of the time we spent making peanut butter and jellies. This time, however, feels more like a big family, the two of us and all the staff, making popcorn. We pass out the snack before the movie starts. The kids have brought blankets or towels, and we all get comfortable and sit on the ground. Fortunately, it is late enough in the season that we don't have to worry about mosquitoes.

For a few hours, I forget about thinking and overanalyzing everything. I let go of all the stress and business that consumes my life and get caught up in the story playing out on the screen. Laughing and cheering along with those watching with me. I also spend some time observing Tate. While I'm sitting on the outskirts of the group, he has taken up residence right in the middle. It's easy to see that everyone likes him, and likewise as easy to see why. He treats everyone as if they are important, sure, but it's more than that. Watching him, it's clear he actually listens when someone talks to him. A characteristic that is getting harder and harder to find these days.

All in all, it's a good evening. In fact, I've enjoyed the entire day much more than originally anticipated.

If there are any side conversations or whispers going on about me and Tate, I don't hear them. I'm not sure if that's because I've been busy doing other things or if Tate had told everyone ahead of time not to talk about such things in my presence.

The movie ends and everyone heads back to their rooms. Tate makes his way to me and asks if I would like to walk to the lake. I look around to see if anyone's watching. Tate, of course, knows what I'm doing, and gives me a reassuring grin.

"We'll be by ourselves, Darcy. I promise." He reaches for my hand, and it hits me that this the first time all day that he has done so. I assume it's because everybody is in bed now. But it does strike me as odd that he didn't do so earlier in the day. Regardless, I take his hand and smile, looking forward to spending some alone time with him.

The full moon is high overhead and Tate knows his way well enough around his property that he doesn't need any additional lighting, though he has handed me a flashlight in case I'd feel more comfortable with one. There's a security gate leading to the lake we stop at so he can unlock. It's the perfect spot for me to overlook the whole of his property and I can't help but to be impressed.

"I just can't get over how beautiful everything is," I say

for what feels like the five hundredth time. "And peaceful. So different from the city."

He unlocks the gate and we continue our walk to the edge of the lake.

"I have to admit," he says. "I definitely find it hard to get used to the city whenever I'm away. And it's such a relief when I pull into my driveway. I think part of it is knowing that this is what I'm supposed to do. It's not like baseball when I always felt conflicted and confused."

"I think it's great that you know with such conviction that you're in the right place and doing what you were meant to. I don't think the rest of us, or at least I don't, have that kind of clarity."

"If you could do anything, what would you do?"

"Oh, wow." I give a nervous laugh. "Going right to the deep questions, aren't you?" I'm not sure I know the answer to what he's asking and if I did, I'm not so certain I want to share it with anyone.

He gives my hand a little squeeze. "Life's too short not to. It's also too short to spend time working at a job that you aren't meant for."

There's truth to his words, but they somehow rub me the wrong way. Seriously, not all of us can afford to walk away from the money he turned down. And I don't think it would make me a bad person if I worked in the hotel industry the rest of my life. Does Tate think Elliott's in the wrong for staying in professional sports?

It would be very judgmental for him to think any of those things, and he doesn't come across as that. But I keep my questions to myself for the moment, not wanting to disturb the peaceful area with an argument, if that is indeed the way he feels.

"I'll think on it and get back with you," I tell him, and he takes it for what it is and doesn't badger me for more.

We had walked by the lake earlier in the day while he showed me around, but it's almost an entirely different place with the lake's surface and nearby pines touched by the light of the moon.

I suppose most things are like that in the moonlight, but there's something magical about the small ripples in the water and the way they sparkle. It's almost romantic, for lack of a better word, if you could in fact say that about a children's camp.

"You talked about your plans for a library and the barn and horses," I say. "What are your plans in general for the camp, let's say three or four years from now?"

He answers quickly which would make it appear as if he has a well thought out business plan. "I actually have a few opportunities for growth." He's speaking more excitedly now. "Especially where the older children are concerned. There are a few companies nearby, both large and small, that have expressed interest in providing internships or summer jobs for the teenagers."

"That is really promising."

"Yes." He nods "It is and it gives them an opportunity to learn a skill or save for college. But to be honest, I'll need to hire someone full time to get a program like that up and running, to organize it, and match everyone up. Unfortunately, I don't have the funds at the moment."

It has to be hard on him, knowing the potential for such a positive program is out there, but not being able to do anything to start it because of lack of money.

"I'll make it happen," he vows. "How can I not when it could change the course of their lives?"

I don't doubt him for a second.

"I've also been asked," he adds. "If I would be able to provide the means for a few people to serve out court-appointed community service time."

"That sounds a bit scary," I say. "How do you know who you're getting to work for you?"

"I spoke to the DA about it, and he assured me that anyone they sent my way would be completely vetted, have a background check and all that. But it's a bit of a concern, so I haven't agreed to it yet."

"But you think you will?"

"I told him I wasn't sure, but I'd think about it and let them know."

I nod, understanding completely. He's in charge of a lot of children and their welfare has to come first. I respect him for that. "What's the plan for tomorrow?"

He smiles. "On Saturdays, the older students interested in culinary arts take over the kitchen and fix breakfast. I know it's not the same as say, working in a five-star restaurant. And it can be a challenge to cook for so many people at the same time. But they learn more than cooking skills; they also learn the value of teamwork."

"They enjoy it?" My mom wasn't much of a cook. I learned at an early age how to prepare a few things, but it's never been something I enjoy.

"They seem to," he says. "Most of them come back the next day."

"You do it on Sundays as well?"

"On Sundays they cook lunch. And if they want, they can also prepare some desserts for the coming week."

Every time I'm around Tate, I grow more and more in awe of everything he has already accomplished. It's impressive. It's also humbling as hell, and I can't help but feel like a loser and a half in comparison. It's not his fault, and he doesn't think that, but still.

We chat a bit more, but not about anything major or earth shattering.

Tate is still holding my hand and every so often he'll run his thumb across my knuckles. I keep waiting for that feeling in my belly. The one I had with Elliott when we were sitting on my couch and his arm was draped across the back. But it never comes. Is it because Tate holds back so much on the physical side? Maybe I need to be more straightforward about what I need in a relationship.

That thought emboldens me. "Will you be joining me in the guest house tonight?"

His eyes widen in shock. Obviously he was not expecting an appearance by Bold Darcy. I'm so certain he's going to say yes, I'm unprepared for his reply. "I hadn't planned on it."

My mind goes completely blank. "Oh," I'm finally able to get out. "I see." I cringe because this conversation makes me feel cheap and dirty but it's too late to stop it now.

"It's not that I don't want to." He reaches his hand out, seems to think better of it, and pulls back. "Trust me, there's little I'd like more than to take you to bed. But ever since I changed my name, I've lived by a set of self-imposed rules and some of those involve limiting any physical relationship, especially here at the camp."

Well, if that doesn't make me feel like a cheap floozy, nothing will. However, he would hate knowing I feel like that. I should steer the conversation away from that direction, but I can't.

"Really?" I ask. "What kind of rules?"

He turns his head and I can't help but wonder if he broke one of his rules by telling me he had them. "Maybe the right word is guidelines. Basically, it's things I either don't allow myself to do or I do them in moderation. I rarely drink. I try never to be in the spotlight or to be the center of attention unless it's directly benefiting my work here. And one of the big ones is I take things very slow when it comes to physical relationships. Especially here on camp property."

I think back to when I did my first internet search on him and what little information was out there after he left baseball. I'd always assumed it was because no one was interested in what he did. After hearing his words about being the center of attention, I wonder if it wasn't Tate who put a stop to all the media. If perhaps maybe the attention he received after turning down that big contract affected him more than he lets on.

Beside me, his body is stiff. I take the hint.

"That makes this weekend a lot easier then," I say.

"Why is that?"

"It kind of takes the pressure off, you know? Knowing nothing we do will lead to anything more physical." But even though he nods, I get the feeling he doesn't. Or maybe he does and I'm just in a rotten mood after our conversation.

It's not too long until we head back to the guesthouse. Tate gives me a rundown of the next day's activities and I smile and tell him I'll be there. The entire time I'm standing there wondering what in the world is wrong with me. Why am I not madly in love with this guy?

Any woman would be completely insane not to be in love with this man. He is absolutely perfect. Smart. Accomplished. Gives back to the community. Devilishly good-looking. Polite. Nice. I'm sure he has a body to die for. And yet he doesn't do it for me. I don't think it has anything to do with his hesitation to get physical. That he has rules is different, even if my first reaction is disbelief.

My heart races as we say good night and he leans forward for a kiss. But it's not the good kind of heart racing. It's the *oh my goodness he's going to kiss me and I want to crave it but I can't work up any excitement about it* kind.

His lips brush mine, but he doesn't deepen the kiss, or even try to, thankfully. "Goodnight, Darcy," he whispers, and I suddenly recall Elliott whispering in my ear. All at once I break out in gooseflesh and shiver.

I hastily get out my own goodnight and head back into the safety and solitude of the guest house. Once inside, I take a shower, drop a quick text to Elliot, and then curl up in bed with my e-reader. Moments later, I throw it to the side. Reading sexy times isn't working for me tonight. With a sigh, I climb out of bed and walk into the living area where I remember seeing a bookcase earlier.

Fortunately, there are no romances to be found. I look through the small offering and settle on a sociological thriller. Hopefully that will keep my mind occupied and off love, romance, and two very different guys.

Except it doesn't.

By the time I head back to Atlanta on Monday night, I'm completely exhausted—in a good way—but when I'm sitting at work tomorrow trying to keep from falling asleep, my body won't care that it's a good exhaustion.

Halfway home it hits me that when I talk about the weekend with Elliott, I need to clarify that good exhaustion does not equate to sex.

CHAPTER SIXTEEN: ELLIOTT

"TO BURN WITH DESIRE AND KEEP QUIET
ABOUT IT IS THE GREATEST PUNISHMENT
WE CAN BRING ON OURSELVES." FEDERICO
GARCÍA

I'm not a person who is easily surprised. However, it's curious to me that every time I am, it somehow involves Darcy. But I have to hand it to Tate. I think his phone call wins hands down for biggest surprise ever. I'm not exaggerating. If I had been any older, he probably would have given me a heart attack.

It's been two weeks since Darcy's enchanted weekend in the mountains of Georgia with Tate. She returned singing his praises and with a glow that has to be a side effect of love. Every time since then whenever she goes out with him, I feel her drift further and further away from me. I'm not handing it very well. I'm grumpy, can't sleep, and snap at damn near everyone.

So yeah, I'm shocked when Tate calls me. We aren't close friends or anything, but since he's in Darcy's life, for at least the foreseeable future, I have to play nice. It's always been my assumption Tate knows how I feel because he tends to keep his distance when we're in each other's presence. We don't text during the week, either. Obviously, it appears I may have been wrong. Really wrong.

I recognize his number when it shows up on my phone, simply because when I called him to set up the date with Darcy, I entered his contact information then. "Hello, Tate," I say when I answer. "How are you?"

"Doing excellent, Elliott," he says and I have a strong suspicion I won't be able to say the same in a few minutes. Or at least that's why I'm thinking my stomach ties itself into three hundred knots.

"That's good to hear." It's hard to hear him over the pounding of my heart echoing in my head.

"I was calling to let you know how happy I am you set me up with Darcy. I've told you I feel like she's the one, but I have to be honest, I grow more and more sure each time I see her. And I have a question for you."

As soon as those words are out of his mouth, I know three things:

- It's going to involve Darcy.

- I'm going to hate it.

- I'll do whatever he asks because in doing it, I'll be making Darcy happy and that's all I want.

"Sure," I say with more conviction than I feel. "What can I help you with?"

"I was thinking about asking her to move in with me. Not immediately. Maybe after the first of the year." I don't say anything. I can't and he adds, "Or maybe in the spring?"

I want to tell him no, that they haven't been dating long enough for that. But you always hear about those couples who just *knew* within five minutes of meeting that the other person was *the one* and got married two weeks later. You know the ones I'm talking about. The ones still married and telling their "How We Met" story on their fiftieth anniversary to anyone who will listen.

"Oh?" It's the only thing I'm able to get to come out of

my mouth with the image of eighty-year-old Tate and Darcy, blissfully in love and surrounded by two dozen children, grandchildren, and great grandchildren, taking root in my brain.

I want to tell him no because he lives in the fucking sticks and if Darcy moves in with him, I'll never see her.

It's not about me.

I close my eyes against the truth of those words, because is it asking too much to have it be about me for once? I take a deep breath and tell myself I will not act like a petulant toddler. We're all grownups here and I have to act like one.

"Elliott?" he asks, jerking me away from my thoughts.

"I'm here," I reply. "You caught me a little off guard with that one. Moving in with you? You know she works in Atlanta, right?" Surely he's not expecting Darcy to quit her job. I don't see her agreeing to do that.

"I was thinking they would allow her to work remotely," he says.

"She spent the month of June working from their locations in Asia-Pac," I tell him. "I'd say that's pretty remote." It's a smart-ass reply, but I can't help saying it anyway.

"I am very aware of how much and how long she currently travels." He sounds a bit put off. "But she *is* looking to change jobs. She put in the request a couple of weeks ago and she told me she hoped to hear back within the month."

I remember my shock at hearing she had requested a change in position. An unwelcome thought enters my head. "Did she make that request because she's expecting this?"

"No, I don't think so." He pauses for a minutes as if he's trying to decide whether or not to tell me something, but eventually he says, "The thing is, while she was here, I told her about a new opportunity that I would like to pursue. Unfortunately, at that moment I don't have funds to do so, but I had thought that if she were to move in with me, perhaps after a while she might want to resign from the hotel and work with me full time."

Frankly, I can't see Darcy ever quitting her job at the hotel, nor would I want her to. Especially if she was going to move to Timbuktu or wherever the hell his camp is. But had I not at one time thought she would love the work he did with the children, and that it would be something she would be very interested in? When I think about it like that, it only seems logical she would also want to be part of it as well.

The truth of it is I'm just a good matchmaker. Other people's lives, I'm great at. My own? I suck.

It's not about me.

It's not, and it is high time I stopped acting like it. This is Darcy's life, and if she picks Tate to share that life with, I have two choices. I can either accept it and live with her choice, therefore, allowing myself to still be part of her life. Or I cannot accept it and put myself in a position not to see her anymore. That's not going to happen. Ever. Tate is not a bad man, and if he is Darcy's pick, then I have to accept that.

I SPEND the rest of the day depressed. Mentally kicking my own ass for setting the two of them up in the first place. Seriously? What the hell was I thinking? *Here, Tate, take my heart and keep it for your own. Nah, I don't need it, it's just a thing.*

And no matter how many times I tell myself that it was only supposed to be one date, the reality is, the whole thing was completely out of my hands after that.

Just as I'm ready to admit there's nothing for me to do other than accept the inevitable, I wise up. And instead of continuing to mentally kicking my own ass, I ask myself what the hell am I thinking? If I want her bad enough, how can I not fight for her?

Seriously, I'm afraid I'll lose her forever if we decide to become more than friends and it doesn't work. Yet I think it's going to somehow turn out differently if I stand by and let her marry somebody else? I don't think so. The way I see it, there are three options not two.

One, I don't do anything because I am afraid. Basically, this is my entire life, or at least me since I realized I was in love with Darcy. I keep us exactly where we are because I don't want to take a step further and find out we aren't compatible as lovers and then lose her as a friend. It made sense then, but it doesn't make sense anymore. Not after that kiss.

Option two, I let Tate have her. There's no arguing about it, this is what I should do, this is the option I should pick. She gets what she wants and he gets what he wants, but what about me? If I think I'm the best option for Darcy and she's the best option for me, don't we at least deserve the opportunity to decide for ourselves if we might actually end up being the best thing for each other?

Option three, we move forward with that. We give in and walk the path not taken. Let's be perfectly honest, we tried it out on her couch and we both seemed to be enjoying ourselves an awful lot before we stopped.

My heart races as I think about the possibilities. I'm getting more excited than I have in a long time. My heart wants to hope. What once seemed impossible, now appears might happen. Or at least it has the potential to happen. Hope grows inside me and I can't stop it. I keep imagining it. It's so real, I can feel it and imagine it in my head. Hell, my arms feel her in them.

Before I go to bed that night, I have a plan to win her heart. A plan to show Darcy exactly what we would be like together. I plan to tempt her. I plan to tease her. And damn it all, if she wants the same, I plan to taste her.

I'm going to show her exactly what I can offer that Tate never can. And by Sunday morning, she'll be mine.

"LOVE IS NEVER LOST. IF NOT
RECIPROCATED, IT WILL FLOW BACK AND
SOFTEN AND PURIFY THE HEART."
WASHINGTON IRVING

*I*t's six o'clock on a Wednesday night, about two weeks after my weekend visit to Tate's. A cousin of mine is coming into town briefly and she asked if I'd be able to have dinner. Of course I arrive at the restaurant way too early. I sit on a couch in the hotel restaurant's lobby and settle in to wait. As I reach to pull the book I'm reading out of my purse, I happen to look up and see someone familiar walking toward me.

It takes me a few seconds to realize who it is and I'm a bit shocked when I do.

O2.

Alice, I have to call her Alice.

She's frowning as she approaches.

I give her a grin. I honestly don't mind her now that she's not with my best friend anymore. "Hello, Alice. How are you?"

"I'm good." She inspects her nails and frowns. "Waiting for somebody."

"Me, too. Would you like to wait with me?" I gesture to the empty place by my side.

She looks around and takes the spot next to me. "May as well, I'm a little early."

"I'm always early. Character flaw." I say it to try and get a laugh or at least a grin out of her, but she's looking at me funny. Unsure of what to do, I just smile.

"How is Elliott doing?" she asks.

Strange, but it's not until she asks that question, I realize he hasn't seen anybody since he took Kara out on that awful date. Going that long without dating is not like him at all. He always has a woman hanging onto him. Unfortunately, Alice takes my hesitation for something else.

"Is he okay?" she asks, genuinely concerned now.

"Yes, sorry." I wave my hand. "It's just I haven't seen him with anyone lately, or even heard him talk about anyone, and that's kind of odd."

She snorts.

Having expected any answer other than a snort, I look at her and raise an eyebrow. "What was that for?"

"Only you would think that was kind of odd," she says, and I swear there's bitterness in her voice.

"What does that mean?"

"Come on Darcy, you're not that stupid, are you?" She tosses her head. "Really? What, do you get off on pretending like you have no idea what I'm talking about?"

"I assure you have no idea what you're talking about." I'm pissed she thinks I'm lying.

"If you have to have it spelled out for you, I'll go ahead and tell you," she says with a roll of her eyes. I bite my tongue so she'll keep talking. "Only you would think it's odd that Elliott hasn't been dating anybody lately, because it's only you he wants to date."

I want to act as if I didn't hear right, or that I don't know what she means, but I can't. Because as soon she says it, I know she's speaking the truth. It hits me, like I've known all along and was waiting for someone to speak it out loud for me.

Elliott doesn't want a flavor of the month.

Elliott doesn't want me to find him a date.

Elliott wants me.

"Oh, my God," Alice's eyes widen and she whispers, "You really didn't know, did you?"

I can't speak. It's all I can do to draw air into my lungs. I think I shake my head in response to her question, but in all honesty, I'm not really sure. It's suddenly very warm in the lobby and only growing warmer by the second.

I have to get out of here.

That's the only thought in my head I can make sense of, and I repeat it to myself over and over. I stand up and don't even bother to look for my keys. I don't need them. I'll have the hotel call me a cab.

"Darcy?" Alice calls as I walk away. "Are you okay?"

I wave her off as I leave, or at least that's what I think I do. Everything is a blur. I walk the necessary steps to the concierge desk and ask for a cab. The man lifts his head and the way his eyes widen confirm I indeed must look as bad as I feel.

Fortunately, he's too good at his job to ask me what the hell's wrong with me. When my cousin first asked me to dinner and I discovered she wasn't staying at one of my company's hotels, I gave her all kinds of shit. Now I'm thankful she's not because the one good thing about her staying here is that I don't know any of the staff.

I have the sense of mind to send her a text from the cab telling her I'm sick and had to go home. Totally unaware, her reply is quick to tell me she hopes I feel better soon and that we'll catch up the next time she's in town.

By the time I make it to my townhouse, I'm clueless as to what to do. If the situation didn't involve Elliott, normally I'd call him. I can't do that, obviously, and this isn't something I'm going to text Tate about either.

Oh, man, Tate. What am I going to do about him?

I'm not hungry and I no longer feel like reading. I finally decide to take a shower and go to bed at an ungodly early hour. When I wake up, I'm shocked at how easy it was for me to fall asleep. I'm also in a much better mood, because in the seconds before I fell asleep, I decided what I was going to do about Elliott.

Nothing.

THE NEXT MORNING, I can't help but wonder if my realization about Elliott's feelings have not somehow been spread across the city to where he lives. It's not even nine o'clock, I'm only on my first cup coffee, and yet my phone is ringing and it has his number across the display. I let it ring longer than I normally do, and when I pick up and say hello, he answers with, "I didn't think you were going to pick up."

I give a weak chuckle and lie. "Sorry, I just ran back from the break room."

"No worries," he says, sounding a lot happier than he normally does. At least recently anyway.

"It's awful early for you to be this chipper. I normally don't hear from you until you've consumed a whole pot of coffee. What's the occasion today?" I force myself to speak slow and even, hoping I don't sound as breathless as I feel.

He laughs, and it's his real laugh, the one I'm used to hearing, not the one of the last few months. The fake one he doesn't even realize I know is fake. "I'm feeling good, is all," he says. "Can't I do that?"

118

I lean back in my chair. "Of course you can. It's just I missed you. You haven't been in the best of moods lately. I'm kinda shocked at the difference."

"Well, this is the new and improved me." There's a smile in his voice. "The new and improved Elliott."

"Bring him on. I can already tell I like him a lot better than the grumpy one."

I hope he's not able to hear how nervous I am, just talking to him over the phone. It's probably unlikely, but if he does notice a difference, I hope he'll think it's coming from something else. Maybe something work-related. Or maybe he'll think I'm having trouble with Tate. Anything's better than him knowing that I know. I think.

I don't know if I should bring up what O2 said. Or if I should keep waiting for him. Hell, I don't know anything.

"I'm glad to hear that," Elliott says. I wonder what it was I said. But I don't have time to ask before he continues, "In fact, I'm calling to see if you would like to meet the new and improved me." He pauses then, a slight hesitation. But no, that's not it, it sounds more like the hitching of his breath, as if he's afraid or unsure of what to do next.

"Elliott?" Is he going to tell me how he feels now?

"Sorry. Someone came into my office."

That's not the case, but I let it slide.

"Can you and I get together sometime Monday night?" he asks.

"Sure." My heart races. "But if you're not busy, I can get together this weekend."

"You don't have a date with Tate?"

"No, he has something he has to do there at the camp, and I can't go up this weekend."

"I wasn't aware of that," he says. "I'd love to get together with you sometime. As long as you don't mind that Carsen will be coming into town and is staying with me over the weekend."

Carsen is his younger sister, who lives in Nashville. She's two and a half years younger than us and moved to Tennessee about eighteen months ago with little more than her guitar and dreams of hitting it big. Elliott is trying to be supportive, but inside he'd love nothing more than for her to come home. She's crazy good, but everyone is in Nashville and it takes so much more than talent to make it work as a professional artist.

"I haven't seen her since she moved," I tell him. "I'd love to spend some time with her."

"She'd love to see you, too," he says. "She's only been home that one time since she moved."

"Where was I then?"

"I think that was when you had the grand opening in Germany."

"Right." That's one of the reasons I'm trying to get my position changed. I'm tired of always traveling. It feels like I'm missing half my life. Traveling everywhere has been a lot of fun and I'm thankful my job has allowed me the opportunity to do so, but it's time for me to settle down. I've been thinking about it for months, but only did something about it recently. "What's she coming home for? I can't imagine it's just to say hello since she rarely comes back."

"Her best friend's getting married and they're having an engagement party Saturday night."

"Saturday night?"

"Yeah," he says. "We'll have to do something early. Maybe around two or three?"

Since the party was Saturday night, I probably won't be able to spend a lot of time with her which is too bad. Carsen is full of life and so much fun to be around. While we were growing up, usually it was only the two of us, Elliott and me. Carsen was always doing her own thing. It wasn't until she went off to college that we started to hang out together.

"I know," I say. "We could go to that new dairy free ice cream parlor near your place. She's still a vegan, right?"

"Year two," he says. "I'm thinking she's not going to change her mind."

I laugh. "Probably not. Dairy-free ice cream it is."

He grunts. He's not fond of vegan food and only puts up with it because of his sister. "Great, I can hardly wait. Seriously, how is that even a thing? Can you legally call it ice cream if it doesn't have any real milk in it?"

It's so nice to have my Elliott back. The one who jokes with me and is lighthearted. This is who I know. This is the Elliott I'm comfortable with. Don't get me wrong, we've both been through rough times in our lives and we've always been there for each other. But fortunately, grief has not played a large role in our life.

"What would I do without you?" I ask before I can stop myself.

"You wouldn't have anyone hounding you about fake ice cream, that's for sure."

I'm glad his answer is a light and jovial response and not at all deep and philosophical because the truth is, I can't imagine a world without Elliott and I'm not even able to think about my life without him in it. The truth of how lost I'd be without him, strikes deeply, it hurts and that means I need to relook at a lot of things. But not right now.

"Say all you want about nondairy and how it makes fake ice cream, but let's not forget whose sister we're discussing."

"Trust me," he says. "There's no forgetting that."

. . .

THE FAKE ICE cream date on Saturday is exactly as much fun as I thought it'd be. Carsen is still just as much of a character as she's always been, full of life and stories about all the interesting people she's met so far and the even more interesting people she works and lives with.

"You have how many women sharing that apartment?" is repeated by Elliott at least five times.

But as we'd suspected would happen, she has to cut out early to get ready for the engagement party.

"When's the wedding?" I ask Elliott when she leaves and it's only the two of us in the red-leathered booth.

"Sometime next May, I believe," he says. "I'm hoping it'll mean she'll come home more often, but I'm not counting on it."

"It's hard when you feel as if you're being pulled in two directions, isn't it?" I ask, seeing his dilemma written all over his face. "The part of you that wants her to spread her wings and make her own way, even if it is in Nashville, and the other part of you that wants her to stay home forever and never change."

"Yes," he replies, shaking his head. "It's exactly like that. I want her here and I want her in Nashville living her dream. But I know how hard it is to make it in the music industry and the sad fact is, most people aren't going to end up with recording deals. I hate knowing the odds are stacked against her because she wants this so much. I'd move heaven and earth for her if I could, but there's not a damn thing I can do to help her."

He looks so dejected, sitting across from me in the now quiet booth that moments ago was filled with his sister's laughter. I can't help it. I stand up and walk the few steps to his side and slide in next to him.

I put my arm around his shoulder and he leans his head

against mine. It feels surprising good and not awkward, even with my body acutely aware of his. "You *are* helping her," I tell him. "You're supporting her by listening to her and being there when she needs you. You aren't nagging her and telling her what she needs to do because it's what you think is best. You're a wonderful big brother."

"Thank you, Darc," he says, not moving his head. "I really needed to hear that."

"I know you did," I say.

It's both odd and completely natural feeling to be sitting like this in an ice cream shop. It's also familiar and yet different to be holding Elliott this way. From the little things to the big ones, we've always gone through them together. But it's been years since he last allowed himself to just lean on me.

As far as I know, it could be years before he does so again. I close my eyes in order to make certain I remember everything in detail. The heat of his body so close to mine. The feel of his muscles I could trace if I wanted, hidden under the soft cotton of his shirt. The smell of him. That Elliott scent no one else in the world has. It's the smell of happiness and home and acceptance, all mixed with something else I don't know how to label, but I would recognize it anywhere. All that together is the scent of Elliott.

He pulls back with an amused look on his face. "Are you sniffing me?"

"Yes," I tell him and giggle. "And you messed me up. Get back where you were."

He tilts his head. "Okay," and relaxes once more against me.

But it's not the same. Something changed from the time he lifted his head up and the few seconds before he put it back down. He's not quite as relaxed. He doesn't seem as comfortable. I surprise myself by not getting upset at the change, but focusing on the fact that there had been a change. That there was something to change from.

Maybe we can stay this way a little bit longer and pretend it's only the two of us again like we were when we were young, and had no responsibilities, and our biggest fear was the possibility of a pop quiz for something we forgot to study.

Yet even as I think that, I know it's impossible. And to be honest, I don't want to go back to that time or to the person I was then. I like who I've turned out to be and I like where my life is heading. Most days anyway. Love life not included.

Elliott takes a deep breath, and I'm startled to realize he's been thinking about something as hard as I have been.

"Penny for your thoughts?" I ask while wondering if he'll truly tell me what he was thinking or if he'll make something up so he can hide the truth a bit longer.

"I want you to do something for me, Darcy," he says, not lifting his head.

"You know I'll do anything for you," I say, leaning my head a bit, just enough to lightly touch his.

"I was thinking about making another dare with you. But this time it won't involve anyone else. It'll only be the two of us."

His voice is very serious even though I think he's talking about the lighthearted dare when we set each other up. Although seeing how serious things seem to be getting between Tate and me, maybe it wasn't so lighthearted. Either way, the matter-of-fact tone of voice he's using is almost enough to send me into flight or fight mode. My choice for rebuttal is to lighten the conversation.

"Are we certain the world can handle the two of us?" I tease.

"I'm not sure," he says, still all serious. "Not sure at all, but I'd really like to see if it could."

My breath catches slightly and he's shot my *do nothing* plan straight to hell. Does he mean what I think he does or is that simple wishing on my part? I'm too frightened to ask if it's the first and too embarrassed to admit the second if it's not.

But I have to know and this is too important to ignore or to leave open for misunderstanding. I shift back, just a touch, but enough to where he has to move and sit up. The way I see it, we both should deal with this head on.

"Are you suggesting? I mean, are you wanting to ..." Damn this is harder than I thought to get out.

He's looking me in the eyes now. Still as serious as before, but I can't read him. "I know you and Tate are getting pretty hot and heavy. And if you're one hundred percent certain he's the one, tell me and I'll leave it at that. You'll never hear me say another word about it. But if you're not certain..." He stops and closes his eyes briefly. "Spend next Saturday with me."

"Doing what?" I ask, because believe it or not, that's the first question in my head.

He smiles. "That's the dare part. Leave it to me. Let me plan a day for you. For us."

My mind flashes back to that night on my couch, and I can't stop the question that pops out of my mouth. "We're not going to spend the day naked, are we?"

He laughs, but his eyes darken and there's a fire in them that tells me it's something he's thought about regardless of the way he answers. "Not even if you beg."

My mouth goes dry because with those five words, the

only thing in my head is me doing just that. I recall both the conversation where he questioned me on my knowledge of his oral sex preferences as well as feel of his lips on mine when we kissed. With that in mind, spending an entire day with both of us naked seems like a really good idea. I resist the urge to fan myself. "Why?"

His voice drops."Because if we spend the day naked, I won't be able to prove my point."

"Which is?"

"If you spend the day with me and have a better time than you've had with Tate, that'll tell you that you should keep looking because he's not the one."

"Then who is?" I manage to get out even though my mouth completely dry.

He shrugs. "I don't know, but it's not him."

My body goes rigid. Those aren't the words I expected and I don't think they were the ones he intended to say.

"Look at it this way," he hastens to add. "If you can have a better time with someone other than Tate, you should probably be with someone other than Tate."

I want him to insert his name in place of 'someone other than Tate' but he's not going to. At least not right now. I collect my disappointment and force a smile. "Okay. Sure. Count me in. Next Saturday."

CHAPTER EIGHTEEN: ELLIOTT

"IN DREAMS AND IN LOVE THERE ARE NO IMPOSSIBILITIES." JANOS ARANY

"*Y*ou didn't tell her, did you?" Carsen asks as soon as she returns from the party and sees me on the couch drinking a beer.

"Nope."

"Ugh." She throws her purse in an empty chair and acts like she's pulling her hair out. "You're killing me. You know that, right?"

I put my beer on the table in front of me and beckon her. "Come here and let me tell you about something."

She doesn't move. "I have zero interest in listening to your whiney ass give excuses about why you couldn't tell the woman you love how you feel about her."

"Darcy won't watch romance movies with me anymore. Do you know why?"

She's standing beside the couch with one eyebrow cocked and her hands on her hips. "Because she couldn't hear them over you crying your eyes out?"

"Ha ha," I say. "Good one, but no. It's because I kept yelling at the guy to suck it up, be a real man, and tell the girl how he feels."

"That right there is irony come to bite you on the ass."

"Right?"

"You should tell Darcy that. I bet she'd get a kick out of it. Oh, wait. You can't. Because she still doesn't know how you feel."

"The thing is, I didn't know it was going to be so hard," I say, trying to ignore her smart ass comments. "It looks so simple. Tell her how you feel. She tells you. You kiss and then live happily ever after."

She rolls her eyes. "Your point?"

"It's not that easy. And I never understood it until I stood in that spot and became that guy, wanting to say those words, but not being able to get them out. It's too hard."

"I'm sorry, what?"

"It's too hard."

She sighs and sits down beside me. "Here's what's going to happen. You're going to sit there and be quiet while baby sister tells you a thing or two. Listen up because I'm only saying it once."

I nod.

"Who the hell told you it was going to be easy? What fairytale crack kingdom did you get kicked out of that filled your head with such garbage? Of course it's hard. That's why they make all those movies Darcy won't watch with you anymore. It's *supposed* to be hard. You're supposed to work for it, and give your all for it, and do fucked-up shit while trying to make your happily ever after pan out." She's looking at me and I'm not certain what she sees, but she shakes her head. "Damn, you are such a *man*."

I almost laugh, because seriously? Didn't she know that? But I don't because there's a lot of truth in what she's saying. "You're right. I have to tell her." She raises her eyebrow again. "And soon. I have a plan, you know."

But I had fucked that up, too, by trying to make it sound like it was only useful for her to know *someone* was better for her than Tate. I didn't make it personal. Didn't tell her that I was a better choice. But I would.

Next Saturday.

Tate had his plan and I had mine. All things considered, mine kicked major ass. His plan could only look at mine and one day hope to kick as much ass. Even if mine wasn't vastly superior, I had an ace up my sleeve. Our last stop on my plan would easily cinch me the victory.

"Tell me your plan," Carsen says. "The only thing you've told me so far is that it is totally awesome."

"That's not enough?" I ask, mostly joking.

"Not by a long shot."

"We're going to spend the entire day together, doing things around the city she enjoys." I couldn't give her too many details, because I still had to confirm everything with several people. There was one thing I could give her details on, simply because it was going to be amazing. My last stop.

Once, years ago, I was setting up a surprise proposal for one of the Storm's players. The proposal itself was going to take place at the restaurant before, but afterward he was going to surprise her with an overnight to end all overnights. That's where I came in. Well, actually me and Darcy, because once she heard about it, she had to be involved.

The overnight was to take place at the most romantic place in the city, a bedroom large enough for only one couple, built into a tree. In other words, a treehouse for grown-ups. Don't let the word fool you. With a bed made of custom Italian linens and handmade furniture, this is no hangout for kids.

As soon as Darcy saw it, she fell in love with the place. I joked and told her she should book a night just for her. You should have seen her face. She very quickly told me that was the very definition of a sacrilege. She said it wasn't a room meant for only one person and would never think of defiling it in that manner. I thought she took it a bit far, but I always kept her love for the place in mind and planned to share the information with whoever she became serious with.

But I'll be damned if I'm going to tell Tate about it. Hell no, I'm keeping that bit of intel all to myself. Until recently, Tate has been able to chase after Darcy unopposed. That stops immediately. I have years of insider information on her and it's not going to be anything close to a fair fight.

Ask me if I care?

Not a damn bit.

I'm going to use everything I have to make her mine completely and in every way possible.

I'm so caught up in my all-day plan to win Darcy's heart, I've forgotten Carsen is still sitting at my side, waiting for me to tell her the details.

"I still have some things to confirm," I tell Carsen.

She's giving me that side eye she has when she knows I'm not telling her everything.

"I'm not going to tell you everything," I say. "Forget it." I really don't think she'll get on the phone and tell Darcy my plans. However, the horrible memories of my date with Kara are still in the back of my mind. Call me superstitious. I don't care. The day's plans will be known only by me.

"Fine," she says, standing. "Don't come crying to me if you crash and burn."

"Come on, baby sister," I say, using the nickname she gave herself. "Don't you think I know how important this day is? Do you think if I had any doubt about my ability to own it that I'd be asking for any and all help I could find?"

"Just making sure you don't let male pride get the best of you."

"It'll never happen." I'm not sure of everything, but in this, I am.

Because the alternative is unthinkable.

ON THE THURSDAY before our date, I do something I actually hadn't thought about the weekend before. It hit me last night. If the date goes as well as I think it will, I'm not going to leave anything to chance. If she agrees to be mine, the whole damn world will know and they'll know Sunday or whenever we decide to join the rest of the world after our tree house time.

I know exactly what I want when I walk into the jewelry store. You can't be best friends with a woman for almost twenty years and not know her taste in jewelry. Darcy is classic and timeless. She favors simple and elegant pieces. I gave her a strand of pearls for Christmas last year after she mentioned she had to borrow the ones she wore to the Charity Ball. She almost cried when she unwrapped them.

Today I'm looking for a similar response, but a completely different purchase. I will admit, my heart is galloping. I can't imagine any man has ever been in the same position and not felt a bit of excited nerves.

But as I walk toward the case that holds the items I'm here to look over, an amazing thing happens, my heat calms, my breathing returns to normal. I give the woman approaching me a smile.

"Hello," she says, drawing closer. "How may I help you this afternoon?"

I hold out my hand. "Elliott Taber, I called earlier."

Because I know exactly what it has to look like, I called all over the city until I found a place that had what I want.

"Of course, Mr. Taber. I remember your call. I have to say, I'm pretty impressed. I'm not sure I've ever had a man know precisely what he wanted. Especially with so much detail." She gives a small laugh. "You would be surprised by how ill-prepared most men are."

"I don't doubt it."

She collects a box from inside the display case and tells me to follow her. We make our way to a less crowded part of the store where we can talk undisturbed. "As soon as you called and told me what it was you were looking for, I pulled what we had in that collection to make certain it didn't get sold."

"I appreciate it."

She opens the box and my breath catches at the sight of the rings inside.

They are all beautiful, of course. It is a gorgeous collection. No matter though, I look from one ring to the next, trying to locate the one I came to buy. I start to panic a little bit, thinking it's not here after all, but then the lady across from me reaches into the box and pulls out the ring I was looking for.

"I believe this is the one, Mr. Taber?"

It is a single diamond solitaire, classically cut, in a cathedral setting, the standard and hallmark of this particular designer. It is stunning. It's exactly like Darcy would wear. In fact, I'm surprised the style isn't called The Darcy. "Yes," I say and clear my throat, so it doesn't sound as raspy when I add, "That is it."

"Would you like to see some of the wedding bands we suggest you pair with it?"

This entire experience is too surreal. Yes, I'd love to say, but I don't because I want it to be something Darcy and I do together. "Not today," I tell her. "She would want us to do it together."

"You must know her very well," she says. "Most men don't have a clue about wedding band preferences."

"I've known her for over twenty years."

She smiles sweetly, with a knowing look in her eyes. "Do you want to take this home today?"

Minutes later, I walk outside. In my pocket is the most expensive thing I've ever bought, for the biggest risk I'll ever take.

CHAPTER NINETEEN: DARCY

"IT IS ONE OF THE BLESSINGS OF OLD FRIENDS THAT YOU CAN AFFORD TO BE STUPID WITH THEM." RALPH WALDO EMERSON

The Saturday of our date, Elliott shows up fifteen minutes early. Normally, this would not be an issue because I'd already be prepared. However today, for what might be the first time in my life, I'm not ready. I have no idea what to wear for hanging out with Elliott.

I'm only wearing a robe when I open my door to let him in. His eyes widen in shock.

"Holy shit," he says, taking off his sunglasses as if to get better look. "Was the apocalypse scheduled for today and no one told me?"

I don't reply, but turn back to continue getting ready. He's trying to be funny, but I'm mad at myself for not being ready. He follows behind me and then closes and locks the door.

"Are you sick?"

"No." What I am is irritated that he's here and I'm not ready.

"Do you not want to do this?"

"That's not it either," I say, walking into my bedroom,

unable to hide the fact that all my clothes are scattered across the top of my bed. I wasn't sure what to wear.

Elliott is wearing jeans and a tee-shirt, totally casual. No big deal. Just hanging out with Darcy, like always. I don't know why I've been making it out like today means more than it actually does. It's not like it's anything big to him. What was it he said? He just wants to show me that I can have a fun time with somebody other than Tate. He's not doing this because he wants me, or that he doesn't want me to be with Tate. He's just wanting to make sure I'm not making a big mistake.

Sorry, o2.

He's being a good friend to me, that's all. I snatch up a pair of jeans and my favorite white tee-shirt off the bed. If he's going casual, I'm going casual. I'm such an idiot to allow O2 to have me thinking he wants more than what we have now.

Elliott is waiting in the hallway. He sees the mess on my bed, but he's kind enough not to say anything about it. As I walk past him, he puts a hand on my shoulder to stop me.

"Hey," he says, and I stop, but I don't look at him. I clutch my clothes to my chest in order not to give anything away. "Darcy." He lifts my chin with his finger and his eyes are worried when I finally look into them. "Today's about me and you, okay? Nothing to stress over, I promise. And I'm sorry if I came across as a jerk. It's only that in our twenty-some-odd years of friendship, I've never gotten ready for anything before you did. You're damn lucky I didn't run a victory lap or two around your townhouse."

He's so serious when he says that last part and I can't help but grin because it's so easy to picture him doing just that.

"That's my girl," he whispers, and I think he may lean

over and try to kiss me, but he pulls back and nods toward my clothes. My skin misses his fingers. "Go get dressed so I can take you to breakfast. I'm hungry."

"READY FOR BREAKFAST?" he asks when I emerge from the bathroom ten minutes later.

"Starving." I flash him a grin and we're off.

I have to admit, I was a bit worried when Elliott first said we'd start the date with breakfast. I'm a hearty eater and I've never hidden that from him, but I feared that if he saw this as a "date" he might try to impress me with a fru-fru fancy breakfast and that is so not me.

I'll never forget when a new five-star hotel opened a few years ago, and Elliott and I went by to check it out. We'd made our way through the very impressive lobby and crossed over to the one restaurant they had to look over the menu. Elliott took dinner. I took breakfast.

"Are they serious?" I had asked. "Eleven bucks for a grapefruit? They mean more than one, right?"

But as we pull into the parking lot of my favorite diner, I relax and realize I never should have doubted him. It's comforting he knows me so well. Especially when he looks at me and says, "I called ahead. They're having all you can eat grapefruit today."

We're still giggling as we're shown to our table.

It's been so long since Elliott and I have the chance to have breakfast together, I'd forgotten how nice it is to order anything I want and not have to worry about getting the side eye from anyone. Not that I typically care what other people think about what I eat, but for business meetings I try not to stand out.

And Tate. I realize with a start. I tried not to stand out when I was around Tate.

With Elliott, I don't care. He's seen me at my best, my worst, and everything in between. So much of my life's story is intertwined with his. How much of the person I am today is as a result of him? Likewise, how much of who he is can be contributed to me?

"What are we going to do today?" I ask between bites of scrambled egg.

There's a sparkle in his eyes. "After this, I thought we'd go to Piedmont Park."

"Really?" At his nod, I add, "I haven't been there in ages."

"I thought you'd like to go. It's your favorite," is all he says. "I have reservations for lunch at that new French place. But if you think it's too fancy, we can cancel and go somewhere else."

I don't think he's joking, but wow, that place is the current hot spot in Atlanta with a waiting list a mile long, even for lunch. "Cancel?" I ask. "Are you crazy? I've been dying to eat there."

It's then I glance down and remember how we're both dressed. I look up at him, getting ready to ask him why he let me wear this when he knew where we would eating for lunch, but something isn't adding up because he's dressed the same.

"Don't worry about it," he says with a mysterious grin. "I have everything under control."

"What does that even mean?"

He pops the last bite of buttered biscuit into his mouth before answering me. "Trust me when I tell you it's going to be fine." I must still look unconvinced because he leans close. "It's my responsibility to take care of you today. Let me prove I can. You're all mine today."

My heart almost stops and as I look into his eyes, those eyes I know so well, and I want nothing more than to be his. And not just for a day. "Okay," I manage to say through the cotton that has taken up residence in my mouth.

"Thank you, Darc."

It's at that moment the private serenity surrounding us is broken by our waitress asking if we need a refill of coffee. Elliott is nothing but utter calmness telling her that we're fine and thanking her for asking. I, on the other hand, am nothing but chaos and wondering how I'm going to make it through the next seven hours.

I NEARLY LAUGH when Elliott pulls up to our next stop. "You really did bring me to a park." I get out of his car. I'm grinning from ear to ear and I don't even care.

"Did you doubt me?" he asks. "How long has it been since you've been to one?"

"So long that I can't remember exactly. Years, I'd guess." I look behind my shoulder and he's walking to catch up with me. Good Lord, I could spend the entire day watching the way his body flows as he moves. His hands are empty and that doesn't make sense. That's when I notice the backpack he's wearing.

"How long are we staying here?" I ask him. He won't tell me what we're going to do if I ask him directly, so maybe this indirect approach will help.

"Until it's time to get ready for lunch," he answers, proving he knows what I'm trying to do.

"It might have worked," I mumble under my breath.

What did work is what he's set up. Almost an entire

morning, all to myself, doing anything I want. It's unheard of. And I love it. I wish I'd known we were coming here, I'd have brought my e-reader along. Reading in the park is one of my favorite pastimes, one I haven't done in ages.

We stop near center of the park at the base of tall leafy tree. He slides the backpack off his shoulder and it drops to the ground. Silently, he unzips it and pulls out a blanket. He glances up at me and I take it from him. Once he's cleared the spot as much as possible, he takes a side of the blanket and we spread it out under the shade of the tree.

He sits immediately. Right in the middle, but I'm still standing and admiring the view. It's an oasis in the middle of the city, and nothing could make it better. Not the weather. Not the time of day. Not the person with me.

"Darcy."

I look down to find Elliott reaching for me. I take his hand, expecting to sit beside him, but instead he pulls me to where I half fall, half sit on his lap. Doing so almost knocks us over and we both laugh. I can't help but compare it to how things are between me and Tate. Well, me and Tate and his rules. Guidelines. Whatever.

I feel free when I'm with Elliott. I tell myself it's because we've known each other so long, but I can't help but think there's more to it than that.

I'm hoping Elliott's going to kiss me, but that seems less and less likely. He sitting there with his eyes closed, and his face is tilted up slightly in order to feel the sun. Taking his hint, I lean back into him, and do the same. Everything about the moment feels right.

"Are you okay?" Elliott asks, which makes me wonder what I did to make it appear as if I wasn't okay.

"Did I say something?" I don't remember saying anything.

"No." He shifts a little bit to reach for his backpack and get something out. "I was wondering if you'd like this?" He's holding my e-reader.

I'm sure I look like a fish, with my mouth hanging open and trying to close it the way I am. "How do you... what is..." I'm so shocked, I can't get a sentence out.

Elliott places the device in my hands. He brings his fingers to my mouth and gently presses his forefinger against my lips. His eyes are filled with an emotion I've never seen in them before. "Shhh.... Just read, Darc. I knew you'd want it."

Of course he does because he knows me so well. It's what I told him that night right before the whole dare thing even started and exactly what he confirmed and told me in return. That was part of why I wanted to see what it would be like if we could end up being something more than friends. But I don't think that's going to happen. The realization cuts deep and hurts more than I thought possible.

For today what we have will be enough. I turn on my e-reader and it opens to the book I was last reading. I lean back against Elliott and start to read. I'm not sure how far I've gotten when my eyes start to feel heavy. I try to keep them open, but it's a useless battle. Closing my eyes, I finally succumb and drift off to sleep.

In my dream, there is no one with me other than Elliott. It's just two of us and he is finally kissing me. His lips are just as sweet, and his kisses are just as addictive as I remember. Maybe even more. He holds me tight against him, so tight I can feel his heartbeat. It is racing, matching mine.

I mumble his name over and over. Each time the only answer I get is his hand stroking me. But that's not enough.

It's not even near being enough. I want him closer. So close he can feel me burn for him. I want him to touch me where I ache for him and to fill me where I'm empty.

"Darcy." He calls my name softly and there is nothing in his tone that sounds urgent or needy. It's way too gentle for what I want. "Darcy."

It's not dream Elliott speaking to me, it's real Elliott. *Shit.* I open my eyes and find him watching me with a curious expression.

"What?" I ask.

"Sorry I had to wake you up. You were having a dream." He glances around the area we're at. I hear the faint murmurs of people nearby, but not with enough clarity to determine where they are sitting or how close they are to us.

Elliott leans down and whispers in my ear, "You were getting a bit loud, and even though it sounded like an amazing dream, I don't think this is the best place for you to be having it."

It's hard to concentrate on his words, especially when my mind is more interested in his breath against my skin and heat of his body so close to mine. He exhales, and I shiver as the warmth crosses my neck. My nipples pebble because his teeth are *right there* and I remember the way they felt on my neck. I want them on me again.

I may actually verbalize that thought.

Elliott jumps up as if something bit him. Even when I stand, he keeps his distance.

"What in the world, Elliott?" I ask, trying not to show how personal I took his action or how much he's hurting me.

"I'm sorry," he says, and I know my attempt to cover up my feelings failed. "I had to, or else...." He sighed, but doesn't finish his sentence.

"Or else what?" I don't care that I sound pissy.

"Damn it, Darcy." He sighs in exasperation.

"Tell me."

He walks the few steps it takes to stand in front of me, totally obliterating my personal space. There's a hunger in his expression that finds its twin in me. It's so much, it makes it hard to look at Elliott and I dip my head so I don't have to.

But he won't let either of us ignore its existence and he lifts my chin with one hand to ensure I hear what he whispers, "I had to move. Being so close to you...fuck, I don't think I can control myself right now. And I don't think you want half of Atlanta to see me ravage you."

Oh God, yes. "I'd prefer not to do it front of half of Atlanta," I manage to get out because his eyes burn me with the knowledge that every word he just said was true.

He nods as if I'd proven his point and turns to walk back to the car, but in fact, he has no idea how wrong he is.

"Not the first time anyway," I add.

He stops and turns around. Slowly. "What was that?"

"I don't believe I stuttered," I say, making my voice as flat as his was when he delivered the same line the night we spoke about O2.

My words pull him to a dead stop, and his face dissolves into something a lot lighter, but somehow just as intense. He's actually smiling when he says, "We need to go if we want to eat at that French place and not get turned away at the door."

If he wants to drop the subject there, I'm not going to pick it back up. At least not yet anyway. Although, if he thinks it's going to remain that way forever, he better think again. I'm allowing us both the opportunity to have some fun, no matter that I'm fully aware how miserable I think he is beneath that mask he won't take off. Even for me.

But that's okay, let him think he's hiding something from me. Let him think I'm not aware of the different masks he uses. I know him so well, I can get him to take them off without him even knowing he's doing it. I smile. That's how well I know him and how good my plan is.

There's only one problem with my plan.

I know everything about him, except for how he really feels about me. And I have no plan on how to get to the bottom of that question once and for all.

My smile dissolves as I realize maybe I don't know him as well as I thought I did.

I'm LOOKING at my jeans when Elliott pulls into the shopping center where the French Bistro is. He said to trust him and I'm trying, but we're here now and my clothes are not acceptable for where we'll be dining.

Elliott is oblivious. Or at least it appears that way. There's a lightness and a joy to him that I haven't observed in a long time. Seeing it today has proven just how long it's been since he's looked so carefree.

He opens the car door for me and I'm getting ready to remind him about our clothes, when what he said to me the first time I brought up what we were wearing comes back to my mind. About him taking care of me because I was his for the day.

Those words stunned me then with their mix of confidence, possession, and protectiveness. Even repeating them in my head makes me aroused and longing for his touch in a way I've never experienced.

It's for that reason that I don't mention our clothes when he takes my hand and leads me...in the complete opposite direction of the restaurant. I can't believe he doesn't know where it is. There are a number of signs pointing to where it is

I catch a glimpse of myself in a window as we walk past and I cringe when see my hair. Damn, and I don't have a brush in my bag because I distinctly remember taking it out the weekend I went to Tate's camp. I'm not able to hold in the sigh that escapes my lips.

"Almost there, Darc," Elliott says, and I bite my tongue so I don't reply back with, "Going where?"

Just as well, because even if he'd told me, I probably wouldn't have believed him. I'm speechless when he leads us into an upscale spa, almost hidden away in the park-like landscape.

He walks right up to the prim and proper woman working the reception desk and says, "Elliott Taber and Darcy Patrick," when she asks for his name.

Within seconds, we're ushered into the back and met by another woman.

"Mr. Taber," she says, "I believe you know where to go?" He nods his confirmation and she turns to me. "Ms. Patrick, if you'll follow me, please?"

Before I can move to go with her, Elliott takes my hand and pulls me into his embrace. "I told you I'd take care of you, didn't I?"

"Yes," I whisper at the truth he speaks.

"I would always take care of you," he says, or at least that's what I think he says. He kisses my forehead and adds, "Go get ready for lunch. I'll be in the lobby when you finish."

I turn to the woman quietly waiting for me with a smile on her face.

"He's something else," she says with a hint of wistfulness.

"That he is." And how did I not notice it before now?

"This way please, Ms. Patrick," the lady says and I follow her into a large private dressing room. There's a small loveseat as well as a wardrobe, and a freestanding full-length mirror. "Your lunch outfit is hanging inside the wardrobe." She points to a door in the far corner. "There's a private bathroom through that door. Once you're dressed, use the phone on the end table and dial 521. Then you'll be escorted to another room to have your hair and make up done. Mr. Taber will meet you in the lobby. Let me know if you need anything. Just dial 0." She slips out of the room without a sound.

I'm stunned speechless. I have to hand it to Elliott, he's really hit the ball out of the park on this one.

I glance at the garment bag in the closet and decide it's best to wait until I see what's inside before making a call on whether he's hit a home run or not. Is the outfit something from my closet at home or something new altogether? I'm thinking it's probably from my closet. Elliott has never gone clothes shopping with me and I doubt he even knows what size I wear.

I would have thought wrong.

The sundress hanging in the garment bag is definitely not mine. But I recognize the cut and the fabric of one of my favorite designers. This is all proof that men are listening and paying attention more than what we give them credit for. There is even more proof when I take the dress out because it's my size exactly. As are the shoes in the bottom of the closet.

After dressing, I stand in front of the full-length mirror in a corner of the dressing room. I need to call so they can start on getting my hair and makeup done, but I had to check out myself first. I'm not one to gloat, but I have to admit I look pretty fabulous. The sundress must be from the designer's new line because I haven't seen it. Which leads to one question:

What's Elliott really up to?

I know what I want him to be up to, but I fear I'm too close to the situation to be objective. I can't let myself believe it's what I want it to be and I can't fathom asking Elliott. Not after the way he's acted the last few weeks and the way I've been with Tate. Especially when paired with a few of the things he's said today. He's the king of mixed signals and I'm the queen. This entire situation is crazy wild.

What's even more crazy wild is the way my heart is racing after my hair and makeup are complete and I'm standing at the door that leads into the lobby, trying to work up the courage to open it.

I tell myself it's stupid and that it's only Elliott and that we've been friends for years and years, and there is no reason to be nervous at simply seeing him. I'm not sure I totally believe it, but it's enough to give me the strength to move forward.

He's standing and looking out of a window on the far side of the room. I push the door open fully and walk into the room. My heels click against the marble floor. Elliott lifts his head at the sound and he slowly turns around.

The suit he has on is one I haven't seen before and the shirt is almost a perfect match of the blue in my dress. His hair is casually messed up in a look relatively few men can get away with, but that makes him look like sex on a stick. But best of all are his eyes and the way he's looking at me, almost like he's never seen me before.

"Darcy," he says, with a shake of his head. "You are incredible."

I give him a sultry smile. "You should know since you picked everything out yourself. I had no idea you had it in you."

His smile is genuine, but that doesn't stop his words from stealing my breath. "There's a lot about me you don't know."

I'm trying to wrap my brain around this new side of Elliott and it hits me. He's *flirting* with me.

I'm such an idiot I could smack my head. Seriously, had it been anyone else, absolutely any other man on the planet, I would have picked up on it instantly. But it's an action I'm not expecting from my best friend, so I'm slow to recognize it for what it is.

Now that I have, the question becomes, will I flirt back? *Duh.*

I walk until I'm standing in front of him and I put my hand on his bicep. His muscle tenses under my touch, but I don't stop. I let my fingers trail up his arm, and I ask, "Are you offering to tell me these things I don't know?"

His eyes flash with a combination of need, want, and surprise, but he doesn't answer. That in and of itself is a surprise. However, his silence only spurs me on. I lift up on my toes to whisper in his ear, "Or would you prefer to show me?"

CHAPTER TWENTY: ELLIOTT

"MY WEAKNESSES HAVE ALWAYS BEEN
FOOD AND MEN. IN THAT ORDER." - DOLLY
PARTON

*S*he's trying to kill me. Or at least give me a heart attack.

Do I want to show her? Can she not feel my dick? Does she not notice how my hands are in tight fists so I don't grab her and do exactly that? Hell, yes, I want to show her. In great detail. Several times. And then repeat.

But here's the funny thing. Okay, funny's the wrong word, but at the moment, it's all I've got. The thing is, the longer this date goes on, the worse I feel. I can't explain it, and it doesn't make any sense to me. But as we keep on progressing closer and closer to my big surprise at the end of the night, I keep feeling like I'm doing something wrong. That spending all day with Darcy the way I am is wrong. That we're somehow cheating.

I should be happy that Darcy is flirting back with me. Heaven knows I like her hands on me. For some reason, however, it seems like something we shouldn't be doing. It's a different feeling than the one I had when I was on her couch kissing her, although it has the same vibe. In this case, I also have that twinge you get in the pit of your stomach when your mind is trying to tell you to stop doing something.

I'm fighting it. I'm fighting it with every damn thing I have. Because I want this, I want Darcy. And the way she's looking at me right now? She wants me just as bad. I'll be damned if I'm going to give her mixed signals. Not now, not when we're so close to becoming everything we can be. Not when we're so close I can almost taste and touch it.

"I'd love nothing more than to show you," I say, lowering my voice in case anyone is listening. "Unfortunately, we have lunch reservations."

She groans, but takes the hand I hold out to her and we make our way outside. Maybe after I eat, that unsettled obnoxious ache in my stomach will go away. I doubt it, but hope springs eternal.

THOUGH SHE DIDN'T WANT a fru-fru breakfast, I knew she wouldn't feel the same about lunch, especially once she knew where I'd made reservations. The bounce in her step and the soft smile on her lips prove how right I am.

She looks gorgeous in the dress I picked out, but then again I thought she looked just as nice in the tee-shirt and jeans she had on earlier. Though there is no way she'd ever step one toe in the restaurant we'll be eating at with jeans on.

There's not a line waiting for a table when I open the door for Darcy to enter. They are strictly reservation only. I called in a favor from one of the players, not the one with the bogus football tickets, and was able to secure us a nice table for two.

Because of all the traveling she does for work with a lot of it involving international travel, Darcy is somewhat of a foodie. She'd never admit it, not even to me, but when it comes to any sort of non-American food, she's picky as hell. Not that I can blame her. When you've worked in a country for one or two months, you tend to walk away with a different palate than the average person.

Darcy has been to France three times, twice for an extended stay. To say she has an opinion on French food is a bit of an understatement. Typically, I can tell in about ten seconds whether or not she'll enjoy the food at any given place, simply by watching her read the menu. I don't even bother to look at mine. I'll know what to order by observing her.

Her eyes light up as she reads over the menu, and that alone tells me this place is a winner. *Take that, Tate.*

"What are you thinking about getting?" I ask.

She bites her bottom lip but doesn't lift her head from the menu before answering. "It's a toss up between the scallops and the chicken. They both sound so good. I could go either way."

"Why don't you get the scallops and I'll get the chicken, and we share?" It's that easy. Darcy gets to try both entrees and since all of my knowledge about French cuisine comes from her, I wouldn't know what to select anyway. Win/win for both of us.

When our server stops by to take our order, he speaks in heavily accented English. Darcy switches languages and orders for both of us in flawless French. I have to stop myself from puffing out my chest in pride and announcing that she's with me. The gentleman taking the order is pleasantly surprised and after he writes everything down, Darcy asks him a question I'm guessing isn't about food. They speak for a few minutes before he leaves to put our order in.

"This place is amazing," she says before I have a chance to speak. "How did you manage to get a reservation? Last I heard the waiting list was miles long."

"One of our players is from the French Mediterranean and his cousin is an owner here." I send up a silent prayer of thanks that this favor didn't blow up in my face like the football tickets.

"It's been so long since I've had real French food. Thank you."

"No thanks are needed. Seeing you happy is all the thanks I want." I chuckle. "I'm just glad this place lived up to its reputation and passed The Darcy Test." Before she can argue with me that there is no Darcy Test, I ask, "What were you and the waiter guy talking about?"

Her face turns pale. "That was rude of me wasn't it? I'm sorry. I should have thought before going off in a language you aren't fluent in."

Her reaction catches me off guard. "You know you're talking to me, Elliott, right? I mean, we have met before."

"I know it's just that..." She dips her head for a second before lifting it back up and meeting my eyes. "But today's different. You know, this is like a date date and some would say it was rude of me to do that."

She doesn't have to explain any further about what caused her reaction, and I could kick myself for forgetting. About eighteen months ago, she returned home from an extended stay in Germany. Not long after, she went out with a new guy. He thought he'd impress her by taking her to a German bistro and instead got angry when she spoke German to the owner. I told her then the guy was an asshole and I still think it today.

"Darcy." I take her hand across the table to make sure she's looking at me and hearing what I'm saying. "Your intelligence and your fluency in multiple languages don't intimidate me. I promise. I actually think it's hot."

"You do?" she asks as relief settles in her features.

"Yes, I'd prove it to you but since we're in an upscale restaurant, you're going to have to take my word on it." I lift an eyebrow and she nods. God help me if I ever get my hands on that guy who took her to the German bistro. "Will you tell me what you two were talking about? Because if he asked you out, I might have to take it up with the management."

She laughs, which was my intent. "No, it wasn't anything like that. He was telling me how his nephew is part owner here and asked him to come help because they're so busy. He's only been in the country for a little over a week."

And it is my super smart, super hot date that is able to be a bright stop in his day by speaking a bit of French.

UNFORTUNATELY, lunch does not settle my stomach the way I hope. In fact, after we finish, we sit at the table and talk, and I think it's actually worse than it was before. Probably because it has food in it now. Food tasting like cardboard and dropping to the bottom my stomach like a pile of rocks.

Darcy, however, seems unbothered by my ailment. She finishes everything put in front of her and part of mine. With a laugh, she tells me that she would lick the plate if she wasn't in public. Just as well, it probably wouldn't be a good idea for me see that live and in person based on how body parts further south than my stomach react just hearing her talk about it.

I glance at my watch and it's time for her next surprise.

"I thought since we were dressed up and everything, we should make the most of it."

She regards me with a thinly veiled curiosity. "Really?"

"Really. You know there's a play in town?" Not just any play. Rather it's her most favorite play ever. The one we saw in New York while we were in high school and the one she played the soundtrack to over and over and memorized every line of.

Her eyes light up briefly before falling again. "Yes, but it's been sold out for months and months."

I reach into my pocket and pull out two tickets.

"Oh, my God. Who did you kill to get those?"

CHAPTER TWENTY-ONE: ELLIOTT

"SOME OF US THINK HOLDING ON MAKES
US STRONG; BUT SOMETIMES IT IS
LETTING GO." HERMEN HESS

*T*hankfully, no one had been murdered in the procurement of our tickets.

I didn't buy any when they went on sale because Darcy's usually traveling this time of year. But as I was planning the day and saw it was in town, I knew we had to come see it together.

Good luck with that, everyone told me.

Like I ever give up that easily.

The owner of the Storm is good friends with the gentleman who owns the theater. This is a tidbit I've known for years, but never worked it out to my advantage. Until recently. After a meeting not long ago, I mentioned my quandary to him, namely, that all the tickets for today's show were sold out. He patted me on the shoulder and said not to worry. An hour later, he was able to hook me up with the owner who not only got me tickets, but a pair of seats in the orchestra section.

Darcy is beside herself when I pull into the theater parking lot. Once inside, she gives me big hug, and hurries to find our seats. A good idea, I believe, because there's not much time until the play starts. I take my seat next to her, looking forward to getting lost in the play. It doesn't happen that way, though, and by the time it's over, I'm more at odds with myself than ever. Being with Darcy might be the right thing, but I'm going about it all wrong.

I do all I can to hide my unease from Darcy, but she's looking at me strangely, so I guess I'm doing a piss poor job. Fortunately, for me at least, it's time for her next surprise, so she doesn't have a chance to ask me anything.

When the owner of the theater found out how much Darcy loves the current show, he arranged for her to visit with the cast backstage after the final curtain. It's not very long after the curtain drops that there is a theater employee standing in front of us and asking for us to follow him. Darcy looks back at me and smiles, obviously delighted. Such a small action and yet, it heats my entire body.

The cast members are warm, friendly, and inviting. Darcy can't stop smiling and takes selfies with everyone. I have a feeling they would have spoken with us longer, but they had to prepare for the next show. Even so, Darcy is still on cloud nine as we leave. It kills me that I'm not.

She turns toward me as we walk out of the theater and gives me a hug. "Thank you, Elliott. This has been an incredible day."

It's getting dark by now and according to my plan, time to head to the treehouse. The staff there will have dinner for us whenever we decide we want it, but I don't expect to order it anytime soon. I think about the ring I bought, waiting for me hidden away in a drawer where it will stay until I'm ready to ask Darcy the most important question of our lives.

I tell myself it's only nerves I'm feeling and that it's completely normal. I'm almost convinced when Darcy's phone alerts her to an incoming text. She grabs her phone, reading whatever it is with a puzzled expression and when she looks up, her cheeks are flushed.

"It's Tate," she says. "He came into the city to surprise me tonight, but I'm not there." She hurries to add, "I didn't tell him I was going out with you today. I probably should have because he wouldn't have driven all the way here if he knew I was with you."

I don't tell her he would have if he had any idea what was next on my agenda.

"Let me text him back really quick and let him know where I am, that I'm with you, and I'm not sure when I'll be back." She bites her lip. I imagine she's quietly berating herself for not telling the guy she's dating that she had plans with another man tonight, regardless of the fact that he's her best friend.

With that thought, I have to do the unthinkable. The thing I've said before that I was doing or was going to do, but never really did. I reach out and still her hand. "Darcy, wait."

She stops, but the question is in her eyes. *Why?*

"I can't continue this anymore." I swallow. "Today wasn't about me trying to see if you should be with someone other than Tate. It was me trying to get you to pick me over him. Over anyone, to be exact."

Her expression relaxes a bit and she smiles. "I knew that."

I'm not surprised, really. Between the two of us, she's always been the smarter. "Maybe," I say. "But you don't know where our next stop was."

"No," she admits.

"I was going to take you somewhere for a very romantic night. At a place no one knows you want to go to except me.

The tree house you love so much. And once we were there..." I shake my head. "It doesn't matter. I should never have gone about it the way I have. If I wanted you to see me as a viable alternative to Tate, I should have made it clear that's what I wanted. Going about it this way, makes me feel dirty and I don't want that for you."

She presses her lips together in thought. "I see."

I'm not sure what I expected her to say, but it for damn sure wasn't that. I clench my fists, determined to get this next part out, even though my pulse pounds so hard, I'm nearly shaking.

"I love you, Darcy. And not like a friend. I've done a piss poor job of showing you, but that's because I've been scared. Hell, I'm still scared, but I'm more scared at the thought of you walking away from me tonight and not knowing how I feel about you." I pause and take a deep breath. I need to finish. "Tate's a good man, I knew it when I picked him for you. He'll treat you right. You'll be happy." I almost say that's all I've ever wanted, but I can't. I wanted a hell of a lot more than that.

She's texting something back to him and I let her this time. I've said all I have to say. What happens next is up to her. I hold my breath when she looks up from her phone. Her eyes are wet and I hate myself for those tears she won't let fall in my presence.

"I need to see Tate," is all she says, delivering the final punch with five small words.

SHE WON'T LET me take her home. She insists on calling a cab. It's just as well, if Tate is still at her house, I don't want to see him. I'm sure the feeling is mutual. Neither Darcy or I speak as we wait for her cab. She stands at the corner, sniffing every so often, each sound is a dagger through my heart.

I did that to her. All this is my fault.

She mumbles something that might be a goodbye when the cab pulls up. My response catches in my throat, so all I can do is wave.

Once she's pulled away, I walk to my car. My revised plan is to drive home and drink until I'm numb. Except, I have to stop by the treehouse because I left the ring there. I'm not sure what I'm going to do with it now that it's not going to be on Darcy's finger. Taking it back is not an option. God, how embarrassing would that be? But I can't leave it at the tree house either.

There is nothing in this world I want to do less than to go alone to the place I had planned to propose to Darcy and then take her to bed. I have to go, but it doesn't have to be right now. I drive, going nowhere in particular, or at least I think that's what I'm doing until I find myself parked outside the place where it all started: the hotel the Charity Ball was held last year. The place I was at when I realized I was in love with Darcy.

If I try, I can remember it. If I close my eyes, it's like I'm there again.

The line in front of us isn't moving, and even though we're in Atlanta and in the south, December can get chilly here.

"Are you warm enough?" I ask Darcy. "I can give you my jacket. It's black. It matches."

"I'm fine," she says and I almost joke that she is more than fine. She is damn *fine. But then I remember we're stopped because of a child and I shouldn't say damn in front of child or anywhere that might be within hearing range.*

I don't actually mind the cold. The press is all over this moment and that can only be good news for team. The big athlete and the small little boy. I notice no one next to us has a camera or phone out capturing it from our point of view. I left my phone in the car because I hate carrying it around, and the only person I would want to talk with is Darcy, and she'll be with me all night.

But I'm willing to bet she has her phone. More than likely it's in the black clutch she's carrying. I'll get it and take a few shots. I turn around to ask her to hand it to me and instead my world stops spinning.

Darcy isn't the least bit interested in the little boy. She's giggling at a little girl who looks a lot like the boy and is probably his sister. Darcy and the baby are playing peekaboo. The little girl cackles in that way only babies can and Darcy is...

She's a walking contradiction. She's all elegant and finely dressed but she's bent down and playing with a baby. The wind blows a bit and a piece of her hair dances in its wake, free from the confines of the delicate upsweep its supposed to be part of. She is the most beautiful woman I have ever seen. But it's more than her looks.

She's playing with a baby and ten minutes ago she was sitting in my car arguing with a man in Spanish about a problem she had with one of her company's hotels. And I don't know a lot of Spanish, but I know enough to recognize when someone is having their ass handed to them and that's what Darcy was doing to him.

She is sexy and smart and I've known her almost my entire life and never realized what I had.

I'm the biggest idiot on the planet.

.   .   .

I OPEN my eyes knowing if I could have a redo, I'd do it all differently, or at least that's what I tell myself. I'd tell her that night. Looking back, I'm not sure what I thought I was doing by not telling her. I pound the dash with my fist. There's no point in replaying the past because there's no way to change it. All I can do is to hope for the best and that when all is said and done, Darcy will still let me be part of her life.

Saying goodbye to my hopes of what might have been, I turn the car around and head into the future. First stop, a treehouse that will forever haunt me.

IT'S NOT A LONG DRIVE. I remember thinking that was such a good thing when I first booked the room. In my mind, my overactive imagination warned me it would not be a good idea if it took too long to get to where we were going. Of course, at the time, I had also anticipated both of us being blind with lust.

Now, I find the drive much too short because I am not able to think. I hope I don't run into the owners. Maybe they won't find it strange if I never request dinner, although it's probably too much to hope they won't notice we're not staying tonight.

From where I park my car, it's only a short walk along a winding path to the treehouse. I try to clear my mind, make it a blank slate, and not to think about anything other than getting in, getting the ring, and getting out. I open the door slowly, unable to keep from noticing how everything has been set up to the exact details I'd given when I made the reservation and again this morning when I stopped by to pick up the key.

Don't think about it now, I tell myself after I look at the bed I had so many plans for.

Fuck, this is going to hurt like hell when I process everything. But I can't allow that to happen until I'm home with a bottle of something to ease the pain.

I search for the ring box I'd placed only hours ago, but what feels like a lifetime away. I find it exactly where I left it. I slide it into my pocket without sparing it a glance. I stay where I am for several long seconds, kneeling by the bed and trying to find the strength to stand up and walk away.

It goes without saying, this is not how I imagined my departure from this room happening.

Don't think about it now.

I sigh and stand. Time to put this dream away forever.

Footsteps sound on the walk outside. The owner, I guess, coming to check and ensure everything is as it should be. I groan and prepare for the looks of shock I'm sure to receive when they see I'm alone.

Whoever it is doesn't knock, but opens the door.

What in the hell?

I'm all prepared to ask the idiot at the door what the fuck their problem is, when they step inside and the words catch in my throat, because I'm pretty sure I'm imagining things.

CHAPTER TWENTY-TWO: ELLIOTT

"LOVE IS COMPOSED OF A SINGLE SOUL
INHABITING TWO BODIES." ARISTOTLE

"*D*arcy?" I whisper. I hate to do anything that will disturb the silence, but I have to know if she's real or not. She's standing in the doorway with a bit of light fog creeping in behind her. For all I know she's a figment of my imagination. She's so stunningly beautiful, standing there with the faint light of the moon bathing her slightly, it's all I can do to breathe.

"Yes," she replies, almost as if saying *Were you expecting someone else?*

I wrinkle my brow, not liking how I can't see her expression. "Why are you here?"

She tilts her head, but instead of saying anything right away, she steps into the room and locks the door behind her. More symbolic than anything. I mean it *is* a treehouse. If someone wants in bad enough, that lock isn't going to stop them. She walks to where I'm kneeling and sits on the bed, just a bit off to my side. Surprisingly, she looks much better than she did the last time I saw her.

By that, I only mean her eyes aren't red and wet anymore. She appears much better after talking with Tate.

She *did* talk to him, didn't she? And she still hasn't said why she's here.

Why is she here?

"Darcy?" My voice cracks.

She's looking down at me from her place on the bed. She gives me a shy smile and lifts her hand as if she's going to touch me, but she hesitates and drops it back to her knee. "Where else would I be? You said this was our next stop."

What she's saying doesn't make sense. But then again, neither does her being here. "Since you said you had to talk to Tate, I assumed you'd be with him."

"You thought...." She shakes her head, almost as if she's thinking I'm the one not making sense. "You honestly don't know, do you?"

I can only frown at her.

She laughs, which I think is a bit mean, and stands up. "After all this time and after all you've always said about how well you know me." She offers her hand to me. "Come up here."

I stand and I admit, her smile captivates me. "What?"

She's facing me and holding onto both of my hands. Can she feel them shake? "I had to talk to Tate so I could tell him I couldn't see him anymore."

It takes a second longer than it should for me to understand what she's saying. A faint flicker of hope ignites in my soul. "You did?"

"I should have told you, but the only thing I could think about was how he drove all the way here and I had to get to him to let him know." She glances away briefly, uncertain for the first time since she walked in the room. "I couldn't move forward with you without letting go of him. You understand, right?"

164

She let go of him to be with me. She wants to be with me. "I'd have understood if you told me."

"You actually thought I'd pick him over you?" She asks as if it's the most nonsensical thing she's ever heard.

"Didn't we discuss how we should only be friends?"

She laughs again. "It cracks me up how you planned this amazing day, yet at the end of it, you still go back to that." She puts her arms around me and I can almost feel that spark of hope ignite into a roaring fire. "Let me tell you very clearly so there is no chance of misunderstanding. I love you, Elliott. I love you as my best friend, but I love you in every possible way a woman can love a man. And I want you in every way as well."

It's hard to pull air into my lungs because of the impact her words have on me. Words that for so long I never thought I'd hear. Words I still find hard to believe, even though she is standing before me and saying them.

She is standing before me and saying them.

"Darcy," I say as the truth sinks in and hot tears of joy, relief, and love fill my eyes. "God, I love you. Don't ever leave me."

"Never," she manages to get out before I claim her lips in a kiss.

I pull her closer, holding her to me tightly, needing the direct physical contact as confirmation that she's here, she's mine, and this is really happening. Kissing Darcy is incredible. If I took the five best kisses I'd had that weren't with Darcy, added them up, and multiplied by ten, they still wouldn't come close.

To have her body pressed against mine is intoxicating. Being able to feel her breath catch and her heart race. To not only hear her moans of pleasure as I run my hand along her side, but to taste them, is the biggest turn on I've ever experienced. I manage to pull away from her a bit, just enough to talk.

"You know," I say. "My plan was to get you here and then to seduce you."

She teases the hem of my shirt with her fingers. "Lucky for you, I don't need to be seduced. I'm telling you right now, you can have me anyway you want, for as long as you want."

"Can I get that in writing?"

"I'll do you one better," she says. With her eyes filled with mischief, she takes half a step back and unzips the back of her dress, all while looking at me. Slowly, she slides one shoulder out, followed by the other. And then I almost forget how to breathe, because the dress slips off her body completely and reveals she's not wearing a bra.

She is so perfectly beautiful, I should probably be still and enjoy the sight of her, but I can't. I have to touch her. Two steps and she's in my arms. Four, and the back of her knees are against the bed.

"Tell me now if there is anyone else you need to speak with tonight." I have one hand in her hair the other is cupping her breast. "Because once we're on that bed, there is nothing else in the world other than the two of us until morning."

"I only need you," she whispers into the skin of my neck. "Only you."

I lift her up and put her on her back on the bed. "You've got me, Darc." I make easy work of my shirt. "In fact, I'm afraid you're pretty much stuck with me forever."

She moves up to where she's reclining against the pillows. It's a position that allows her to reach me easily and I suck in a breath when she trails a finger across my chest. "I think forever is a good place to start. You have the most amazing chest. I've always thought that." She flashes me a smile. "I've always wanted to do this, too."

I don't have a chance to ask her what she's talking about because, before I can formulate a response, she's pushed me down and is leaning over me. "Darcy?"

"I've always wanted to know how you taste."

She dips her head and licks me. How it's possible that her licking my chest can send a jolt of electricity to my dick I don't know.

"Mmm," she hums, moving her mouth further down my body until she gets to my belly button. "Even better than I imagined."

I'm starting to think it's entirely possible I may not survive a night with Darcy in bed. But when she begins her southward exploration and tugs at my pants, I make her stop. "Not right now."

"But I didn't get to taste everything I wanted," she says with a slight pout.

"Later," I promise because believe me, there will be a later. "First, there's something I've been wanting to do. Or rather taste. Do you remember the conversation we had the night you made the first dare?" The soft flush of her cheeks says all I need to know, but I want more. "Tell me."

"Yes," she says. "Of course I remember. Hard to forget something like that."

"Then you know what I want to taste." I don't wait for her to acknowledge anything. "Go face the headboard, hold on to it, and crouch." My dick is about to explode at the thought of finally getting my mouth on her. She pushes the waistband of her panties down, but I stop her. "Leave them. They play a part in my fantasy."

White cotton. Exactly what I'd always assumed.

CHAPTER TWENTY-THREE:
DARCY

"WHATEVER OUR SOULS ARE MADE OF, HIS
AND MINE ARE THE SAME." EMILY BRONTË

J'm pretty sure I'm in a dream.

I brace myself for the alarm that's bound to go off in the seconds before Elliott touches me. The bed sinks, though, as he moves, and I don't ever remember dreams being that detailed. Which means this is real and everything is finally the way it should be.

I would weep with joy if it wasn't for the fact that I'm so aroused I'll probably lose it the second he touches me. The bed moves again and his breath is warm along my inner thighs. My hold on the headboard tightens at the feel of his fingers on my skin.

"Look at this." He traces the middle of my panty from front to back. The cotton is damp.

"Your fault," I somehow get out because he keeps stroking and it feels so good, my eyes are about to roll to the back of my head.

He chuckles and the vibration tickles me. "I suppose since it's my fault you're in this predicament, that I should take care of it." Ever so slowly, he pushes the cotton to the side, and I whimper at the way his fingers brush across me.

All it takes is his mouth on me and I'm so primed, my body shatters with release.

"Holy shit," I say, when I can talk because that was the most intense orgasm I've ever had and he's barely touched me. I expect him to stop with the foreplay since I've already climaxed once, but he keeps on. "Oh my, God." I'm close to grinding myself on him and all I want is him in me, now. "Elliott, please." I shift so I can get down on the bed, but he stops me.

"What are you doing?" he asks.

"I've come already; you don't have to keep on doing that. We can move on."

"That's good to know." He places a kiss on my inner thigh and then looks up at with a wicked gleam. "However, I'm not finished enjoying you like this."

I swallow, because, holy hell. "I just figured it was something you felt like you had to do. Not that it was something you necessarily wanted to do."

He dips a finger inside me and removes it. "See this?" At my nod, he continues. "This is what I do to you. This is how I make you feel. It means you want me. You're attracted to me and your body is preparing to have me inside it. Call me arrogant or prideful, but I love the fact that I have that effect on you. So like I said, be still, I haven't finished with you like this yet."

I can't argue with that and, to be honest, I don't really want to. "If you insist," I say with a fake sigh and getting back into my previous position.

He snorts at my response, but if I'd thought I had the last word in that discussion, the joke was on me because I have two more orgasms and my underwear is long gone before he pulls away and helps me get back on the bed.

He's completely naked by this point and though I'm

sated from all those orgasms, he's the complete opposite. His cock juts up, clearly in need of attention. I'd love nothing more than to return the favor and take him in my mouth. He's long and thick, and I think it's only fair for me to have my turn.

Either he's reading minds now or else I'm licking my lips, but I catch Elliott's eyes when I'm able to tear my gaze from his erection, and he's shaking his head. "Not this time."

He's also ripping a condom open and I'm not about to argue with what that means. I settle back on the bed and watch as he gives himself a few jerks and rolls the condom on. He looks up and gives me a lopsided smile. "Enjoying yourself?"

It's then I realize my legs are spread and I'm teasing myself with my fingertips. "Not really. It'd be better if you were over here with me and helping."

Two heartbeats later, maybe three, and I'm in his arms and he's kissing me. "I love you, Darcy," he says between them. His words are soft and sure, and when I look into his eyes, I see the truth of his words.

I run my fingers over his mouth. If I could, I would grab those precious words and hold them in my heart for always, for I will never tire of hearing them. "I love you, Elliott." I lift my hips because his cock is driving me to the brink. Seriously, it's *right there* and I want it so bad. "Please don't make me wait any longer."

He relents and positions himself at my entrance. "Look at me." His voice is rough, yet when I meet his gaze, everything falls into place.

We had talked about needing more from our dates and as he pushes inside me, I realize I only needed more from Elliott. I needed this. Him. As more than my best friend.

More than the guy I've known forever. The doubts I had with Tate are not present in Elliott's arms. Everything finally feels right.

"That's because it is," Elliott says. He's holding back, hardly moving at all.

"I didn't know I said that out loud."

"You didn't." He flexes his hips and enters me fully with a hard thrust that takes my breath. "I just know."

I'm too far gone to think anymore. For now, my world exists only as me and Elliott. There is no hesitation, no awkwardness. It's as if our bodies have known all along what it took our heart years to figure out.

Hours LATER, my head is on his chest and he's running his fingers through my hair. We're nowhere near being finished with each other for the night, we're simply resting. The white lights in the tree sway gently. It's the most perfect night I've ever had and it's hard to imagine that this is only the beginning.

"I wish we had realized sooner that we were supposed to be together," I say. "Think of all that time we wasted."

He drops his head down to kiss my forehead. "I don't think we were meant to know it until now. I think all our past experiences brought us here. I'm not sure it would have worked out if we tried in college or something." He pauses for a minute. "I didn't know then that I was in love with you."

I prop myself up on an elbow. "When did you know?"

He talks about last year's Charity Ball and the little girl with the sweet laugh that I played peek-a-boo with. I'm stunned.

"I can't believe you knew this entire last year and didn't tell me," I say.

"I had to come to the point where not telling you was the worst thing I could do and realizing that telling you might be a risk, but that it would be worth it."

"Would you still think it worth it if I hadn't felt the same?"

"Yes, because my love isn't dependent on you loving me. It's only dependent on you. And loving you is everything."

The sincerity in his expression is so real, I feel it in my soul. I pull him to me. I need him again. Need to show him without words how much I love him and that love is always worth the risk.

But he doesn't budge. "Wait," he says. "I forgot I had one more thing I wanted to do today."

"Elliott, I love you, but you are out of your mind if you think I'm getting out of this bed to go somewhere right now."

"Lucky for you, you can stay right where you are."

I cock my head. "I'm not overly thrilled about you leaving, either."

His grin is full of mischief. "I'm not going anywhere."

I'm lost and a little confused, but nod. "Okay, then. What was it?"

He slides out of bed, and completely naked, gets on one knee and holds out a ring box.

My hands fly to my mouth, because surely he's not....

Not while he's naked.

While we're both naked.

He's still smiling. "Darcy Patrick, will you marry me?"

Oh my, God. He is. And I don't care. "Yes," I say, reaching for him and this time he's letting me. My lips are on his and his are on mine.

"Wait." He pulls back. "You haven't even seen the ring yet."

I don't care what it looks like, but I let him open the box anyway. As soon as I see it, I'm glad I kept quiet because it's the most perfect ring ever. "Elliott," I say as he slips it on my finger. "It's gorgeous."

"Not as gorgeous as you are." He's looking at me and all I see is love. He tucks a piece of my hair behind my ear. "I could sit here and stare at you all night."

"The bed would be awfully lonely without you."

He gets that playful look I know so well and sits down, naked, in a chair. "Let's see who can last longer before they reach out for the other person."

"You're not going to last long at all."

He crosses his arms. "I'm not? You're the one talking about the bed being lonely. I think you'll cave first."

I laugh because he really doesn't know me as well as he thinks and I can't believe I'm able to pull this off a second time. "I need you to come kiss me, Elliott." He shakes his head. "Come on, *I dare you.*"

He's off the chair and on the bed before I blink. "You're going to pay for that," he growls, taking me in his arms.

I run my hands over the expanse of his back. "I certainly hope so."

He's kissing me the way I'd asked for, and I no longer worry about my future because Elliott will be with me. Together we will be unstoppable.

EPILOGUE: ELLIOTT

"IT'S DELIGHTFUL WHEN YOUR
IMAGINATIONS COME TRUE, ISN'T
IT?" L.M. MONTGOMERY, ANNE OF GREEN
GABLES

*W*hen we were freshmen in high school, the daughter of a mutual friend of both of our families got married. The wedding was held at an old historical house and to say Darcy fell in love with it is an understatement. She's never been one to talk incessantly about her wedding, but on those rare occasions it happened to come up in conversations, she always said that house would be the perfect venue.

The weekend after our epic date and engagement, when she mentions having our wedding there, I want to groan. Everyone knows they book years in advance. They won't have anything available for two years, and damn if I'm waiting that long to make her Mrs. Elliott Taber.

Likewise, there's no way I can tell her no when she's had her heart set on getting married there for over fifteen years. I tell her to call and see what they have open.

The smile on her face when she skips into the living room less than ten minutes later is unexpected. I hope to hell she hasn't booked the house for a Saturday two years from now.

She sits in my lap and her smile slays me. It'll kill me, but if we have to wait two years in order for the wedding to be held at that house, we'll wait. If it means that much to her, how can I not?

"What do you think of a February wedding?" she asks.

"Brrr," I say, and pretend to shiver.

She punches my arm. "I'm serious."

"I am, too. It's cold in February." The only thing worse than waiting two years to get married is having to wait two years and still getting married in February.

"They have the second Saturday in February free," she says, and she doesn't have to say who *they* are. "After that, they're booked solid for eighteen months."

Eighteen months? Hell, no. "I always wanted to get married in February."

She raises an eyebrow. "Really?"

I chuckle and run my thumb over her bottom lip. "No, but I want to marry you and if you want to get married in that house, that's what we'll do. If you want to do February, I'm all for it, and if you want to wait eighteen months, I'll also do that. I don't want to wait that long, but I will."

She thinks for about three seconds. "Let's be wild and crazy. Let's plan a wedding in less than four months and get married in February."

"Are you sure?" I ask and I want to kick myself, because what the hell? What kind of crazy fool tries to plan a wedding in less than four months? "I don't mind waiting. It'll be warmer and you'll have more time to plan."

She doesn't answer. At least not right away. Instead, she leans down and kisses me.

Over the last week, I can't count the number of times we've kissed. We've kissed so many times and so many places, it's as if we've been making up for lost time. And still, every kiss rocks my world just like the first kiss we shared on my couch not so long ago.

My head still finds it hard to comprehend that these are Darcy's lips on mine. That she loves me and that my lips are the only ones she'll ever kiss again. Something primitive and fierce ignites deep inside my chest at that thought and I have to pull back because I don't want to start something we can't finish. And as much as I'd love nothing more than to pull her closer and do a hell of a lot more than kiss, we have dinner reservations with some friends soon, and we should start getting ready.

"Is that a no or a yes to waiting?" I ask.

"That's a *you better find the warmest tux you can find because you're out of your mind if you think I'm waiting eighteen months to marry you.*"

I don't try to stop the grin that takes over my face because I know she wants to get married as soon as I do. I give her a one last quick kiss. "Go call them back and book the second Saturday in February."

She leaps from my lap with a squeal, and darts into the kitchen where she's spread out all of our wedding plans on her kitchen table. I hear her excited chatter from my seat and I can't help but smile. I need to pinch myself because it doesn't seem real that this is my life.

A FEW WEEKS LATER, we make an appointment to look at wedding rings at the store where I purchased her diamond. I'm not surprised the woman working there remembers me. She'd said the last time I was here that she'd never had a male client so knowledgeable about what he wanted in an engagement ring. I didn't correct her then and I won't today either. The truth is I don't know shit about rings. I only know Darcy and what she likes and wants.

Crazy how before our engagement I'd never given much thought to wedding bands, or what I wanted. To be quite honest, even now my only thought on the topic is I'm good with whatever Darcy picks out.

"Mr. Taber," the sales lady says, coming up and shaking my hand. "So good to see you again." She looks over Darcy with a knowing smile. "And this must be your fiancé."

"Yes." I put my arm around her. "This is my Darcy Patrick."

"Ms. Patrick," she says. "It's good to see you. I'm Macy and before we get started, I have one question. How did he do on the ring?"

Darcy's beaming as she answers, lifting up her hand to look at the ring there. "Just perfect. It's the exact one I'd have picked out if I to choose."

Macy nods. "I had a feeling you'd say that. He knew what he was looking for when he called initially." She picks up Darcy's left hand. "And it looks like it was made for you. Let's go pick out some bands that match."

The ring does look like it was made for her, but what strikes me the most is the possessiveness I feel whenever it catches my eye. To me, that ring is a flashing light. MINE. TAKEN. DON'T EVEN THINK ABOUT IT. I like to think I'm a man of this century, enlightened, and all that. Funny how a simple thing like an engagement ring can turn me into a Neanderthal in less than two seconds.

Instead of beating my chest and exclaiming, "Darcy. My. Woman." I take her hand and follow Macy to where she has the bands out and ready for us to look through.

It doesn't take long for me to be completely overwhelmed by the variety of bands available. I don't get it.

I knew exactly which diamond I wanted to give Darcy, but for some reason picking out slim band to go with it, as well as another one for me, makes my head spin. What metal do we want or do we want a combination of two? Do we want plain or some sort of design? Diamonds, yes or no?

"I just want something plain," I finally say. "Something simple. Something that when I see it, I'm reminded how lucky I am to be your husband. Something that looks like a wedding band so there's no doubt I'm taken and not interested." I pick up a plain band that looks similar to the metal of Darcy's engagement ring. "Like this."

My breath catches in my throat when I look at it on my finger. This is real. It's really happening. Darcy is marrying me. Me. I try to speak but my mouth won't work.

Darcy places her hand on my shoulder. "Elliott?"

"Definitely this one for me," I manage to get out, but no louder than a whisper. I look up and Darcy watches me with a curious expression.

"I agree," she says, picking up a ring matching mine, and sliding it into place next to her engagement ring. She takes my left hand in hers. "Perfect."

EPILOGUE: DARCY

"ONCE UPON A TIME, THERE WAS A BOY
WHO LOVED A GIRL, AND HER LAUGHTER
WAS A QUESTION HE WANTED TO SPEND
HIS WHOLE LIFE ANSWERING." NICOLE
KRAUSS, THE HISTORY OF LOVE

"*I* don't know what the hell I was thinking, believing I could plan a wedding in less than four months." The big day is a month away, and I'm overwhelmed trying to get everything taken care of. My kitchen table is covered in nothing but lists. It's so bad even my lists have lists.

Elliott comes up behind me and slips his arms around my waist. "What's stressing you out?" he asks, and his lips brush the back of my neck.

I hum and lean back against him. "Nothing at all when you do that."

"Come here," he says, pulling me away from the table and into the living room.

"What?" I ask him when he sits down.

He points to the space beside him. "Have a seat."

My mind is shuffling through all the things I need to take care of in the next few days. "I need to go through the responses and make sure the caterer is up to date."

"I'll take care of it tomorrow."

I see what he's doing. He's feeling guilty because he

181

doesn't think he's helping me at all, so now he's going to take over half my lists. I can't have him do that. It's not that I don't trust his judgment or that I think he'll forget something. I'm just that big of a control freak. "And I need to confirm my dress fitting and my portrait date and time."

"It's after five. Neither of those places are open now."

I sigh. "I know, but I need to put it on the list for tomorrow."

This time, he doesn't ask. He pulls me down into his lap. "Not tonight you're not."

Elliott's not one to go all controlling on me, which is a good thing because I'd probably tell him to go jump off a cliff. But for some reason, the way he takes charge and pulls me into his arms feels really good.

Yet, as good as it feels to be in his lap and arms, I really do have a lot of stuff to do. "I need to make sure everything's in order."

"How about we call the wedding off and go by the courthouse, tomorrow?"

That I think about it for even a second shocks me. The idea is tempting but I can't do it. I've already called in so many favors for this wedding I need to see it through. "As much as I'd like to do that, I don't think we should."

He kisses me softly. "I don't like seeing you stressed out about what should be one of the best days in our lives."

I pull back, just a touch. "Can you honestly tell me you didn't get stressed out planning our epic date?"

"I'm not sure you can compare the two. I was also trying to steal you away from another guy."

"Outside of that, did you have any stress?"

"Did I have any stress outside of the fact you were dating a man who was perfect for you. That I was so scared I might never have a chance to be with you? To hold you and tell you how much I love you? That I would spend the rest of my life thinking I was too late? No, that was quite enough stress." He's trying to keep it light, but it's a struggle. I can't even image how much different my life would be had he not been brave enough to pull off the epic date.

I tuck my head into his chest just because I can and that in doing so, I can hear his heart beat. I place my hand across the steady thump and take comfort in knowing I never have to worry about a life without him.

After a few minutes of being in his arms, my body relaxes. The entire time he keeps holding me, gently stroking my hair. "You're right, you know," I tell him and my head for a kiss. "The most important part of our wedding day is that at the end of it, we're married. Everything else is just icing on the cake."

A strange look crosses his face.

"What?" I ask. "What's that look for?"

"Did I tell you the baker called about the cake?" He looks guilty now.

"No, when did she call?"

"An hour and a half ago."

I surprise us both by smiling and kissing him again. "She can wait until tomorrow. I think we need to discuss something much more important." I stand up and he raises an eyebrow.

"What would that be?" he asks.

I take his hand and lead him into the bedroom. "Sheets."

THE SECOND SATURDAY in February is cold. Or at least the weather is cold. There's nothing about me that's the least bit cold. I spend the morning getting ready. First is breakfast with my bridesmaids. Carsen is there and she tells me Elliott is in a bad mood because he thinks the tradition of not seeing each other before the wedding is stupid.

I can only agree.

The day seems to drag until it's finally four and time for me to walk down the aisle to Elliott. I take a step toward him and it's like everyone else around us disappears and only the two of us exist. He looks more handsome than I've ever seen and he's smiling and it's a smile just for me.

It hits me at that moment how my entire life with Elliott has lead to this point. Looking back, it seems so obvious, it has always been me and Elliott. Today isn't changing that. It's only making it permanent.

I remember one of my friends mentioned that as she walked down the aisle, she made it a point to look at her guests in the eye. Another friend said she focused on the floor runner, afraid of tripping over her feet. I'm not able to focus on anything other than Elliott. If there are guests watching us, I'm not aware of them. If there's something on the floor that could make me trip, I must be lucky because I'm not looking at the ground.

There are two things in my universe: me and Elliott. Once I make it to the front, there are three: me, Elliott, and the man who will make us one.

I speak my vows as if it's the most natural thing in the world, and it is. No matter what happens in the future, we'll always have each other and nothing can ever change that. He's mine. Forever.

And I'm his.

I'd been worried about what I'd say at the reception, but I as I stand in front of our guests, once more my eyes only see Elliott and the words I'd been so worried about come easy.

"We've known each other for most of our lives. From Kindergarten to college, you were always the one I could count on to have my back. In elementary school, you refused to let any boys pick on me on the playground. When I worried about making a fool of myself in front of my high school crush, you're the one who talked sense into me and gave me the courage to ask him out first. When a different boy broke my heart years later, you were the one who sat with me and helped me go through a record number of ice cream pints."

The guests laugh and the crazy thing is, I don't even remember what that boy's name was. He was so important to me at the time. Little did I know how everything would turn out.

I smile at my new husband. "All of my highs and lows and in-betweens have one common thread: Elliott Taber. You've seen me at my best and at my worst. And neither of them have scared you off. You told me you knew you were in love with me at last year's Charity Ball. After you said that, I thought back, trying to figure out when I knew I loved you and the thing is, I can't place a finger on an exact date or time. For me, I think love came quiet and soft. So slow I didn't recognize it and so complete I could never escape."

I take a deep breath because I'm close to crying and I don't want to cry even happy tears today. "You have been my best friend, my confidant, and my lover. Today you also became my husband. You're the only one I see when I think of forever and the only one I want to spend it with."

The room is filled with the sounds of clinking silverware and glasses, but the most precious sound is the one suddenly in my ear as my new husband takes me in his arms and whispers, "I love you, Darcy Taber."

If you enjoyed THE DATE DARE, you won't want to miss
Tate and Carsen in
THE DATE DEAL

Seven years ago, I went from being America's Golden Son
to That Idiot faster than you can say, "Foul ball."

At the time, I thought I was making the right decision
by ditching my professional baseball career and today, I
know I did. But I'll admit, being the punchline of every late
night comic changed me. The paparazzi no longer follow
me and the media's moved on, but I still live by rules created
to ensure I would never be a laughingstock again.

My rules are restrictive and controlling. They dictate
what I do and who I do it with.

They do not allow for a free spirit, bound and
determined to get a recording deal in Nashville. A woman
actively chasing a public life I turned my back on. And they
certainly will not accept the little sister of the man who
recently married my ex.

Unfortunately, this siren with the voice of an angel, is
the only woman I want.

So I made a deal...

THE DATE DEAL

THE DATE DEAL CHAPTER ONE

The invitation arrives on a Wednesday. It would stick out from the assorted junk mail, bills, and letters from past campers on its own, thanks to the heavy cotton of the envelope, but I'm first notified of its presence by the excited chatter of a ten-year-old girl.

"Mr. Tate! Mr. Tate!" she yells, running into my office and sliding to a halt seconds before crashing into my desk. She has the day's mail clutched in one hand, and she's hopping around from foot to foot.

"Gracious, Haley," I say to her, unable to hide a smile at her enthusiasm with today's mail. Her grandmother, Susan, works for me and often, Haley accompanies her. She shoves the envelope my way. "Look at this!"

I know what it is the second my fingers touch the heavy paper. I don't need to read the return address, but I do. *Darcy Patrick, Atlanta, Georgia.* An invisible fist squeezes my heart, but I only allow it to hurt for five seconds. My smile is back in place when I look down and meet Haley's expectant gaze.

"It's a wedding invitation," I say, and point to the return

address. "See? It's from Darcy, a friend of mine. She's getting married."

"Is she very pretty?"

"Yes and smart, too. She travels all over the world with her job."

Haley's eyes grow big. "Wow."

I wait for her to turn and run off to find a new adventure or a group of campers to play with. But she's thinking hard about something.

"Well," she says. "If she's so pretty and smart, how come you aren't marrying her?"

"Because she isn't in love with me."

"How is that even possible?" she asks, with all the innocence of a ten-year-old. "You have the coolest job, ever, and you don't look that old."

I can't help but laugh at why I'm such a catch. "Thank you, Haley."

"This guy she's marrying?"

"Elliott."

She nods, as if she knew already. "Yeah, Elliott. What's he do?"

"He works with Georgia's professional lacrosse team." At least I guess he's still with them. The last time we spoke, he was looking for a job that didn't involve as much travel as his current one.

She wrinkles her nose. "I don't even know what that is."

"It's like a mix between baseball and football, but not really." I'm not sure how to explain lacrosse.

"It sounds dumb. You played baseball and you have this place. She should marry you. *Everybody* knows what baseball is."

Haley's grandmother walks into my office, saving me

from having to come up with other reasons why Darcy isn't marrying me.

"Haley," she says. "What did I tell you about bugging Mr. Tate?"

"I was bringing the mail to him and his friend, Darcy, is getting married, and she's dumb for marrying Elliott instead of him."

I have to hand it to her, Susan is much better at schooling her features than most people. She knows who both Darcy and Elliott are since she was here the weekend Darcy came to visit. Elliott she knows about since I've often credited him for both setting me up with Darcy and stealing her from me.

Of course she's also aware I went out with her daughter, Jane, Haley's mom, a few times in the past before we decided we'd be better as friends. What Susan doesn't know is that Jane and I became more like friends with benefits, but I'm not willing to lose the best admin I ever had over a woman I haven't touched since before Darcy.

Her expression is neutral as she looks at her granddaughter. "Your mother and I have both told you not to call people dumb. Go play outside before I call and tell her what you said."

Haley doesn't hesitate. She spins and is out of my office faster than I can tell her goodbye.

"I'm sorry, sir. Obviously, she doesn't know about..." Susan waves toward the invitation I'm still holding.

"It's okay." I stopped telling her years ago not to call me 'sir'.

Her gaze remains fixed on the invitation as if it's a snake poised to strike at me. I place it on the edge of my desk to deal with later. Much later.

"They're moving fast, aren't they?" she asks.

Darcy broke up with me in November. It's January now and, from what I've heard, the wedding is at the end of next month. Crazy if you ask me. Who gets married in February?

Moving fast? Yes. Especially when you factor in that according to reports I've heard, Elliott proposed the same night Darcy broke up with me. Rumor mill also says he was naked when he got down on one knee. God, I hate that the world of professional sports is just one big happy family and even though I walked away from that family years ago they still accept me. Red headed stepchild they now see me as or not.

Regardless, I don't allow gossip in my presence. Especially about people with active ties to that small knit community. Susan knows this.

I say nothing in response to her statement and she turns and bustles around, picking stuff and straightening up the already spotless room. I wait until she leaves before opening the invitation. The words don't have the impact I feared.

They're getting married in February, just as I thought, but in the garden of a historical home. I put the invitation down. Outside? In February?

Really?

I'll go. There's no question about it, especially since she invited me. I'll book a room for that Saturday night, which means relying on my staff. Not that they're not able to run the camp while I'm out for a night, they wouldn't work for me otherwise. It's just I like it better when I'm here. When I'm in control.

I assume it was Darcy and not her husband-to-be who invited me. She's even addressed the inner envelope "Tate and Guest". Not only is she expecting me to come to her nuptials, she also wants me to bring a date.

I can't help but wonder how many people at the wedding will know who I am?

Not as Tommy Maddox, but as Tate *the guy Darcy dropped for Elliott* Maddox.

It shouldn't bother me what people think. I'm thirty-one and should be well past the age of caring. *Should be.* But I'm not.

Apparently, being the punch line of every late night comedian's joke, the subject of poorly written tabloid headlines, and being portrayed in a skit on Saturday night television, messes with your head. Trust me, it's not a place you ever want to visit and if you're ever unfortunate enough to go there once, you'll do anything in your power not to make a return trip.

Usually, I keep myself in line with a set of self-imposed rules. They felt restrictive when I first made them. Now I've been following them so long, they're a part of me. They weren't strict enough to keep me out of this pickle, unfortunately. That has nothing to do with the rules though. Nothing and no one could have predicted that Darcy would realize she was in love with her best friend of twenty years while we were dating.

Even if their relationship could have been predicted, like if Elliott had been honest with me about his feelings for Darcy any of the four or five times I asked, the ultimate ending would be the same. The one night I drove into Atlanta to surprise Darcy, she'd been out with Elliott all day. I didn't know and when I arrived at her townhouse and found it empty, I sent her a text. That text marked the end of us as a couple.

The thing is, I don't miss Darcy. I miss the idea of her.

I place the invitation back on my desk to be filled out and sent in later. A quick glance at the clock tells me it's almost time to see how I can help with dinner preparations. I may have at one time pictured Darcy as part of the camp's future, but that will never happen.

I, however, am the camp's present, and there's rarely any downtime.

ALSO BY TARA SUE ME

ABOUT THE AUTHOR

NEW YORK TIMES/USA TODAY BESTSELLING AUTHOR

Even though she graduated with a degree in science, Tara knew she'd never be happy doing anything other than writing. Specifically, writing love stories.

She started with a racy BDSM story and found she was not quite prepared for the unforeseen impact it would have. Nonetheless, she continued and The Submissive Series novels would go on to be both *New York Times* and *USA Today* Bestsellers. One of those, THE MASTER, was a 2017 RITA finalist for Best Erotic Romance. Over one million copies of her books have been sold worldwide.

www.tarasueme.com

Printed in Great Britain
by Amazon